Book design by A. Torres

Cover image by Jorge Guillen, from Pixabay.com

KDP ISBN: 9781-0860-66876

Published in 2019

Kindle Direct Publishing

Contact:

atorres@49at67.com

Red Sticker

To Michelle

Thank you for kicking me out of a long-lasting writers' block.

Red Sticker

Alex Torres

Two

I

Confused; disoriented; lost; out of senses; doubtful. So many modes to describe in the simplest form the way she was feeling at the moment, sitting at the top while watching the open road parting by her feet. Not because she didn't know what she was supposed to do, but because she wasn't sure if her heart was in the right place, to begin with: her mind was playing tricks and her memory was not helping at all. Last she remembers is just the jump; the sudden loss of weight and the impotence of feeling without control. Even the fall itself was escaping for the moment from her brain. Did she land properly? Was she in sync with the wind as she was hurtling towards the abyss? Only fragmented images were rapidly flashing, one after the other, with no specific order or sequence that she could identify or put together. Terrified and out of breath, she started looking for a reference point to use as an anchor to her rationality.

She could simply stay put and wait until the sensation went away, but the adrenaline was already kicking in and the desire to run was coming back. The air was thin, fresh and energetic; the rocks were not sharp at all and the pasture to the sides of the route was like those yellow tapes they place at the off-road races so you don't get lost in the run. The path was clear but still, she could feel the urge to calm down and wait, once more. It has been so many times by now for her to be in the same position, under the same circumstances that she has become an expert on controlling the upsurge that comes after every episode. Why would this be different from any other in particular?

What was her direction, after all? To pursue a dream, to provide, to fulfill? She could have done that easily even before the first block. But the push was hard and consistent; persuasive and in a certain way, unavoidable. Sometimes you make decisions, not only for yourself but also for every other life you may touch and affect in your race towards a target. And in those cases, those lives can persuade and mold the outcome without you even noticing what they have done. One can only hope that the consequences do not produce a domino effect, where the chips all fell in the same orderly fashion, one after the other in rapid progression.

She was uneasy; divided; torn. The weight of her wings was too much to handle at the moment and her shoulders were acutely sore. Maybe because they were supposed to carry her, and not the other way around. But disoriented as she felt, it was too dangerous to fly away and was better to stay on land and walk instead. The rhythm of her feet could easily overcome the beating of her heart although not for long. Major decisions have to be made, but not at the moment. Right now, it was the perfect time to contemplate, conclude and then advance when the brain was ready to drive again.

In one hand, she was feeling the need to expand, conquer and convert. Integrate, include and connect with others around her, some awaiting to reciprocate but without the minimal desire to participate. Humankind after all: defects and deviations over uniqueness. The fresh breeze dancing between the feathers across the entire wingspan solidly attached to her back was telling her to let go; to look front and never turn her gaze back.

On the other hand, the cover that the same feathers were offering was tempting, warm and cozy. The invitation to follow the rules was overwhelming. She was created with self-control already built-in, and the instruction manual did not include a section to overpass the master plan that was written in her heart.

She risked a bit of her security and took a quick peek over the border. Just enough to have an idea about what was showing on ahead of her. There was an almost perfect balance between winning and losing, and her head started to hurt just by overthinking and imagining a multitude of potential outcomes. The payoff was worth the gambling and the opportunity was there for her to take. It was just a matter to decide and take action, but the seconds became minutes and the minutes transformed into hours. She was standing still in silence, breathing slowly and trying to look inside of her for the proper response. It was always herself pushing the limit of her abilities and testing her endurance with every trial. It was her own pressure what took her to where she was at the moment and it would be only her again who will take her entity to the next step. She wasn't completely sure about the way to get where she wanted to go, but she was certain that she will be arriving sooner or later, and preferably in one piece, if possible. The goal was clear in her mind, but the incertitude of her actions so far was taking a toll on her heart.

She made a final decision and stood up in one smooth movement that shook the dust from her wings. Her head started to spin both because of the quick movement of her body and because of the rush of electricity on her spine. It was exhilarating to move again after being quiet for so long and the taste of adrenaline was always something to enjoy before a jump. Her eyes were staring forward, her feet firmly planted on the floor and her arms extended as if they were trying to reach to the horizon on both sides at the same time. It was now or never.

One last breath in silence; one final push inside her soul. She contemplated again the loss of contact with those close to her, or that wanted to be close. *"There will be time for that later on"* – was the response she heard from somewhere in her brain – *"There will be always time for that"*.

She closed her eyes and took a step ahead.

II

She wasn't sure what was hurting her the most: the broken ribs, the IV needle deeply inserted on the left forearm or her shattered proud. The run was fantastic and filled with adrenaline in every step going down, but she forgot to master the landing before departure. Who told her that she could handle such amount of energy encapsulated in a tiny colored idea, after all? It was her decision all along although she was tagged by a friend. And where exactly was this "friend" right now? Alone and in silence, she turned her head around and looked carefully but she couldn't find any traces of another racer whatsoever.

There were no colors, and almost no sound; there was no other person around. It was quiet and dark but you could perceive a fainted light coming from below the door, barely making shadows inside the room. And the smell was something you would remember later on if asked by an inquiring mind. It was one of those smells that are not quite disgusting but still could get attached to your nose for the longest possible time. Dry and sharp, a mix of ocean breeze and manure, fresh but filled with a blend of mud and grass. It was like walking thru the forest behind a cattle ranch after a rainy day in May.

She got up from the bed, carefully walking to the door and tried the handle, opening it just enough so she could take a peek outside. More people were visible now, slowly walking in all directions in silence. A few of them had an IV attached to their arms too and they were pulling a rolling post to their side like a lovely companion, dancing under the light features covering the ceiling along the entire corridor. Some were reading a book or a piece of paper that looked like a letter, and some had headsets on them probably listening to their favorite tunes. But nobody was talking to anybody: it was like they didn't even acknowledge the presence of each other. She started to wonder if they were just as lost as she was after a night run, or if they were still swimming in the same ocean as she did just a few hours ago. They all had the same confused look on their eyes, and the way they were moving was a telltale about the condition of their minds if you knew what to look for. She wanted to adventure a little bit to the outside, but she didn't know where to go. It was an unfamiliar place and there were no signs on the walls indicating an exit, a path or anything else that she could use to find her way out. There was nobody around that looked like they were in charge, to ask for directions.

She returned to her bed and pulled the sheets up to her chin, feeling disturbed and confused at the same time. It was a comfortable bed, although it feels cold to the touch and smelled like it was deeply sanitized recently. Her feet were cold too. She forgot to turn the lights on after looking outside but didn't want to stand up again. There was still silence all around her and outside of her room. No sounds were coming from what she could barely identify as a window to her left. It was a strange feeling, hearing nothing but her breathing and her heart, pounding faster with every passing minute that she was there.

She tried to remember how she could have ended in that place, but the effects of the landing were still blocking her memory. She didn't feel remorse, although something was telling her that not everything was alright. There was this feeling of missing something or somebody, but she couldn't pinpoint to what or who was missing from the picture. A feeling of a deep void started to build up inside of her, as she pulled the sheets even more to cover her face. She felt the tension on her shoulders promptly increase when she heard the door's hinges as it was suddenly open, and cushioned steps moving closer to the bed.

Her breath was almost imperceptible as she tried to stay as quiet and immobile as humanly possible, without success. She noticed some shadows projecting on the sheets and heard voices talking to each other while moving around her bed and across the room. She didn't want to see, but her curiosity was gaining terrain and she moved the sheets a little bit down her face. It was dark and the figures bending down over her were frightening enough to make her cover her eyes again. She heard laughs and felt a hand reaching under the sheets and touching her shoulder. She felt a bolt racing thru her entire body, but she was unable to make any type of movement at all. The hand was soft and didn't felt like trying to grab her by force. It was instead very gentle and warm. It was then that she noticed the fact that this felt like a hand from a woman; soft and small.

Her heart was speeding even more but the gentle touch over the shoulder was, to her surprise, making her feel better. She stopped feeling afraid and adventured once more to look over the sheets. There was some light this time, coming from the now open door. It was tenue, but enough for her to see the person that was looking directly to her eyes. She had green eyes, blond hair and a light blue scrub with short sleeves. A stethoscope was hanging from her neck.

"Don't you worry, sweetie. We got you on time. You will be fine" – her voice was melodic and reassuring, but she started feeling a panic attack almost immediately. It was not the woman causing it, but the incertitude that she was feeling about what happened to her.

"I mean, it's not like we don't know you already, right? Everything is going to be Ok".

Her panic was overpowering now.

III

Every other envelope was already open and properly disposed of. The trashcan close to her feet was proof of that. The table was empty except for the corner to the right of the napkin holder. There was still one package sitting right there, big, white, clean and crispy as the morning after coffee. The stamp was from an out of state postal office and the address label was printed, not handwritten. It looked official, and the logo next to the sender information was making it look even more important to her eyes which were glued to that spot like as if it would disappear if she ever dared to look away or even blink for a second or two. She could swear it was all part of a dream, although one extremely vivid and realistic. She got lost for a moment on the memories of past lives and experiences. It has been a wild raid, after all, but with every decision made and every turning point, the light at the end of the tunnel was closer to her. Too painful to revive, she awoke from her memory trip and realize that the soup was getting colder on the stove behind her. It was a moment of genuine terror when she finally moved her gaze and focused her attention to something else, other than the far corner of the table.

Walking to the cupboard, she looked at the window and noticed the school bus dropping kids at the bench installed by the mailbox. Always at the same time and the same spot. Always the same driver for the past couple of years. He was a familiar face by now although they had never met. There was no reason for it after all, as she was always telling herself every time she caught him looking at her from his seat, smiling and nodding with a grin on his face. Laughing and the sounds of running kids were accompanied by the barking of a dog, probably too excited at the sight of them. She wondered again if that location was properly chosen and if those sounds were too scary for a person like her. But it was herself who made the decisions all the time. Nobody to blame; nobody to thank. It was her path and she had chosen right over comfort – or anything else for that matter – whenever was needed. A complete 180 turn was made, some would say, but it was more like a zig-zag across a mined field during the Conquer of Smithy Hill.

She went back to the table and started eating the soup in silence, now that the school bus had left the bench behind. Her eyes were again fixed at the address label on the envelope by the corner, still unopened and still crisp and clean. It will need to wait until her brain and soul were ready and in sync. Too much pain and too much suffering left behind; too many scares, resolutions and resolve built up to this moment. All worth it, all accepted; all forgiven and forgotten. Time will need to adjust to her, and not the other way around.

She wasn't sure yet, but something inside her mind was telling her that the outcome would be positive. And that possibility was way scarier than any other on her mind: there was no going back; not this time.

She thought about that option long before when she started slowing down and made better choices for her life, and she rejected the idea almost immediately. If she wanted to correct her path, she would have to make sacrifices. And that same feeling was not going to stop her from opening the damn envelope right now. She reached out and barely touched it, retracting her hand almost immediately like it was electrified or incredibly hot. Something was not quite right, but again, it never was. She reached out once more and grabbed it by the corner; slowly but surely sliding it across the table towards her.

A few sips of soup later, a very fainted smirk was the only remaining signal of what just had happened in that kitchen. Her eyes were now looking thru the window and onto the future. Too much planning to do; too much to prepare and so little time to do it. But again, time was under her control as it has been for the past few years since the last landing. Her feathers were a little rusty now, but still with enough energy to carry her over to the next block.

The silence around her was evident, the dark from the night was already entering thru the windows and the soup was long gone. She was still sitting at the kitchen with her left hand supporting her tilted head on the side. She noticed that she didn't turn the lights on, but she was deeply enjoying the dusky ambiance in peace. She stood up and turned the radio on. She was always listening to one of those stations that played old music from the era of the great bands. Although some of her friends found that amusing, she preferred that over any type of modern styles. *"It helps me to concentrate"* – she was always telling them. They just smiled and agreed with her without discussion.

The silence was interrupted by the barking of a dog and she looked outside to see if the one that belonged to her neighbors was again outside on the street. She was always catching him during his escapades. She couldn't see him as it was already dark and decided to look around the block. She needed some fresh air anyway.

She went to the living room and took her tennis shoes from the little closet next to the entrance. She was about to sit down on her couch to put them on when the doorbell rang twice. She wasn't expecting any visitors and the sound caught her by surprise. She rapidly put the shoes standing in one foot and then the other and went to the door. As she opened it, the surprise on her face was something worthy of a picture.

She couldn't see his face at first, not because he was hiding, but because her attention was entirely focused on the fresh bouquet of roses on his hand.

One could immediately tell that they were both experienced, although they made it look like it was easier than it was. No book could have prepared them for what was happening in that room, and their purpose was not to show others what they were capable to handle; they simply handle it as required. No rush and no fuzz. Everything under their control as it has been for the past few years since their parallel tracks finally intersected at one point. Although she was more focused than he was, they looked to each other for guidance and support when they needed it. There was a lot of commotion going on around them, and the noise from the machines was not helping at all. Still, it was like a cloak of silence was hovering over their heads since nobody else outside the room was aware of any single word said between them. When all was done and gone, the deafening silence dropped dead over everybody else's head. Conversations started again after a few tense minutes of chaos and a sense of normality was almost perceptible again in every corner of the room. It was a scary moment without a doubt, but they looked at the event more as if it was a learning experience rather than a traumatic episode. Again.

Smiles all around, greetings from visitors that were just arriving or a well-intended goodbye from those already leaving. Lots of flowers and gifts nicely arranged in a table by the corner placed next to a floor lamp. The TV was turned off, hanging above one cold and unfinished dinner brought in from the kitchen, not long ago. She returned every single gesture with the same cheerfully attention, even as she was tired as Hell. This was nothing compared with the past, and he could tell she was ready to sleep. But time was under her control, as always has been. She never said a word about planning and prevention, and he didn't insist on talking about it. There was never time for that, or their spirits didn't want to dance that tune just yet. Still, somehow they both were always ready for the scare if the occasion arises. It was a natural gift on their nature, and maybe that was what connected their paths in the first place.

She finally fell asleep with the sheets firmly tucked under her body and a cozy comforter placed over her feet. The TV set was still off and the silence outside the room was now acutely noticeable to him. No more hands to shake and no more explanations to give. Now, it was just them sharing the darkness and quietude inside, and the fainted gleam coming from outside thru the window at their left side. The curtains were dancing as the breeze moved them in continuous waves, and the street lights started to awake since the night was coming forward. He wasn't sure about the time but in reality, he didn't want to know: sometimes is a blessing to get lost for a while when one navigates a delicate timeline, wandering with no purpose in mind and just walking around to cleanse the soul.

He knew one thing for sure: now that she was losing the battle with the night demons of her darker dreams, she would not be coming back to him without a plan, and not until a few hours later, fully rested and ready to talk. His stomach started to protest and remind him about the smell of coffee that was drifting from the end of the corridor, every time the elevator's doors were open.

It was hard to leave her alone, knowing so well that everything could turn bad in a moment and without a warning. The idea of seeing her walking to the edge was scary like nothing else on their lives. She was strong and dedicated, and she won all her rounds in the past. He was mortified by the possibility of giving up, although this was something he never shared with her. And giving the fact that he had his dance ball to attend, he was terrified by the idea of actually *leaving her alone*. As it was before when he was looking to her from the distance, she was somebody you would not like to mess with. How would she react to a battle of his own? She knew already, and he was always wondering if her recent jumps were caused precisely by that. This was enough a possibility to make him feel doubtful about what to do and how to prepare for the future if there was any.

All of a sudden, he remembers something he saw in the newspaper, and a smile showed up on his face. There was one option available although it sounded crazy at first. But given the circumstances and all of the scares they had over the years, he was open to any suggestion. He would need to validate and confirm, but it was something worth checking out, for sure. He knew already that he was some kind of crazy and still got married under the Moon. Adding one more shenanigan to his curriculum was nothing but an extra checkmark on his bucket list.

He walked away from her bed towards the suggestion of breakfast that his nose was pointing so precisely while trying to make him react, by hurrying him up to leave.

He looks at her, blows a kiss, turns around and quietly closes the door behind him.

V

Not again. Or at least not this time. There may be better windows in the future when they all were already grown-ups and may understand fully the reasons behind her choices, but the demon was already awake and dancing around her feet without a sign of stopping. It was cold as the winter at her first place, when the curtains moved with the gelid breeze that found its way under the door and between the cracks around the windows, and the water heater prefers to get into a tantrum instead of running properly as it was supposed to run. The pain was deeper and protracted, and the medication was just a reminder about a routine that worked in the past. As she slowly opened her eyes and scanned the room, the bright light from outside was a very clear indication that the night would be a prolonged battle to fight. Although she was ready as she ever did, this time something was different. Not distinct enough to notice at the first try, but perceptible if you paid attention to the details: the pain started to be pleasant and almost desirable; the headache was intense but manageable. The adrenaline rush was mysteriously absent and the desire to run was dissipating from her mind with every passing minute that she was there, laying on the bed.

Why keep fighting this time, when she could simply relax and enjoy the jump into the last block? One more decision to make; one more simple risk to take.

After all these years of flying, her wings were just tired old rags hanging from her back. No more morning wind running thru her feathers. No more swimming into the ocean at night, under the moonlight. One last thrust and it would be time to sit down and enjoy a cup of coffee served with homemade cookies, fresh from the oven. She was a fighter, and she would continue throwing punches even if the battle looked like a lost cause. But she was tired as she was never before today. Her legs felt like tatters and her arms were barely moving.

She was thinking about that first time when she was looking down from the highest point and decided to go for the run, zig-zagging from one side to the other as she was testing the trail and the conditions of the ground. Somehow she managed to stay on her feet when a rock interrupted her pace, although her balance was never the same after that.

Even that she was resting on her bed, her mind was making her imagine that she was standing inside her kitchen, looking to the pantry with a confused look on her face. She wasn't sure why she was just standing there motionless, but her knees were no longer able to support her body and she fully kneeled until her hands touched the floor. The weight of her wings was too much to bear. Her head was tilted down and a single tear started to run down her cheek. She stayed down for what it looked like an eternity, as she tried to recover her breath and her senses without success.

"Not again. Not this time" – she started to tell herself as she was trying to regain her will to resist. Her legs were refusing to collaborate, and she was finding harder to force them to move. A deep pain inside her stomach made her crouch down and rest her hands on the floor, in front of her head. She knew this feeling from before, but it was a very long time since the last episode took place. Why was it coming back now?

Her entire body was aching, and her head was spinning around. She felt the desire to vomit, but she was not having it. Not this time around. She wanted to stand up and run outside, to touch the ground with her naked feet, to jump into a river – if there was any around – and swim to the opposite side, climb the river bank and roll on the mud. There was a feeling of desperation and an unmeasurable desire to scream to the top of her lungs coming from her inside and that feeling was trying to tear her apart. She knew perfectly well what was coming next, and she was ready to confront it.

She raised her head again and kept it up while she forced her body to react by pressing both hands against the hard floor. She was now with only one knee down. A deep breath and a pause long enough to gain some more energy on her lower body helped her to finally stand up. She felt sudden dizziness and reached for a chair to sit down and regain her composure. The desire to vomit was back. Knowing that she would need some time to recover, she closed her eyes and started to focus on her breathing.

When she opened them again, she was back on her bed, resting sideways with her back to the window. She couldn't see it, but she felt the cold on her spine and knew immediately that a few hours have passed already since she was gone.

The spinning floor sensation disappeared but the aching on her body was still with her. There was a sentiment of emptiness taking over, and as she stayed still she felt exhausted. Her energy was drained and her will to continue was pale in comparison with a few days back.

Why keeping fighting? Why continuing pushing herself with every passing day? She was a warrior, but even a fierce combatant sits down sometimes and wonders. Was this one of those times for her?

She moved her feet together and crossed her arms in front of her. It was her favorite position. It made her feel secure and comfortable. It was like this how she imagined everything could end someday: in a quiet room, alone, resting at ease in bed.

And this was better than the alternate scenario that she saw before.

VI

He walked back into her room and immediately noticed the sideway posture opposing the open window to the left. He has seen this before several times and was very well versed on the significance concerning her backstory. She was not facing the night coming inside, now that dusk was saying hello with a dark smile; she was curled and relaxed, breathing slowly while keeping her eyes shut and her arms firmly embracing a body pillow. She didn't even react when he touched her shoulder and ran his hand to her hips under the sheet. He was worried about the state of her mind at that moment, but he was sure she could handle it pretty well, as she did it before. It was just a matter of time for her to come back from whatever situation her brain was having her at the moment.

She was warm to the touch and comfy to the eye, barely moving with every heart beep amplified by the monitor connected to her fingertip. He didn't want to wake her up, but the desire to kiss her was bigger than reason, as it always was the case between them. Slowly, he bent over and placed his mouth close to her ear, while his hand removed the hair just enough to clear her neck. He kissed her but she didn't move or respond to him.

Smiling, he completely understood what she was doing. He was with her during her first and every episode after that; he was resilient at first but become very supportive as he learner her reasons with time. It was not that he supported her decisions, but he understood why she took them. Comprehension was a very delicate line that not everybody wanted to cross, but oddly enough this line and their continuous dance around it was precisely the reason for her to grow so deep on him. She was delicate to his eyes, a rose in a garden full of thorns. As he always said to friends and relatives the first time they meet her: *"It was not that she was petite by accident; it was just that God ran out of materials to complete the rest of her after finishing creating her heart"*.

Looking at her face for a reaction, he noticed a subtle movement of her eyes, even as they were still closed. He touched her earlobe with his lips as he quietly said, like many times before: *"Where the fuck you think you're going?"*.

He moved his head away and looked again to her face, waiting with a composed attitude. It was kind of silly on his part, but he wanted for her to wake up by herself, knowing very well how mad she would be if he dared to interrupt her even on this moment. Especially at this moment, to be precise. He crossed the line before, and the experience was something he didn't want to repeat ever again.

She opened her eyes and turned her head to him; she felt a yearning for the house next to the school bus stop.

"*If only you knew*", she thought in silence, coincidentally responding to his question from before, either without even knowing, or because she heard him asking his question while she was fighting to recover her presence of mind.

Still smiling at him she suddenly realized that her dancing demons would need to wait, whether she liked it or not, probably until the arrival of the next block.

Twelve

"Why is everybody moving so much around me? And why am I just laying down here in the middle? I want to play the same game too! But they are not calling me; they are just looking at me with the same face they do whenever I do something they don't like and they keep touching me all over my body. I don't like that a bit. I prefer the other face, the one they do when we are out in the fresh, running behind each other. I like that face a lot.

But they keep moving and pointing to my legs, and I don't understand why. I know that they are bigger than me and can move faster than me now, and I try my best not to stay behind, at least most of the time. Some are smaller, but I don't see them here. Maybe they are outside playing without me. I would love to go and look for them but the last time I tried to move they placed their hands even harder over me as they tried to keep me immobile. And it hurts a lot when they do that.

One of them – the one I don't remember seeing before – has something in his hands, but I can't see clearly what could that be. And this is another thing: I don't know why but I can't see properly anymore; it's like somebody have put something in my eyes. Like the time when we were playing in the water. But in that time it was only for a moment that I lost the view of them. Now it does not want to go away, everything looks blurry and

I can't understand why. And my eyes hurt too, just like my legs.

Mom is talking to him. I can tell that they are talking because I can overhear their voices although I can't understand what mom is saying. I can hear, but I can't make sense of the sounds. It is a very weird feeling not being able to tell what they are saying. Are they talking about me, about what happened? Maybe they are but I can't be sure.

I think I need to stay quiet and try not to move again. It seems that they don't like it when I try to move and attempt to stand up. And I don't like it either, especially because it hurts. But I want to see where the small ones are. I miss them a lot. We play together every time they come back after lunch. I see all of them leaving when I wake up, and then coming back home after I am done eating, and I always greet them at the door. Sometimes I greet them outside when mom lets me go to the porch, and I make sure they can hear me from far away and recognize me over the others.

Something I don't understand is why they leave after I wake up, although there are some times when they stay at home too. And I like those times a lot because they spend almost all day playing with me. We go outside for a very long time, and then we come back and have lunch together. It's funny how mom gets mad when they share their food with me, but they do it anyway. I can eat by myself quite well, but I like it a lot when they give me some of their food and I try to give them some of mine and we all laugh together. They put one of those faces that I like a lot when they do that.

But right now, mom has the same face she usually makes when she catches us sharing our meals. She is looking now to the door but she is staying in the same spot, next to me, standing in silence. Is she leaving me here, or taking me back with her? I am starting to feel panic just thinking about what she will do next. The ones that are bigger than me went outside too, maybe to join the small ones in their games. I want to go too; I want to play with them all even if I can't follow them around as I used to do it before. I know that I move slowly now and got tired very quickly, but I still want to go with them. If I got fatigued, I can sit on the side and watch them play until I can join them again. It will take some time, but I will catch my breath again.

I don't want to stay here alone with the one that I don't recognize. It can't be good to me that he has something hiding in his hands. She better takes me with her if she's planning to leave!

She's looking at me again, but she's not talking to me. It seems that she's listening to him while he is showing her some papers. Hey! Maybe he drew me and he wants her to keep the drawing! I love it when others make drawings like that. I know that mom has some that were made by the small ones, and I believe that I look fantastic on them. They showed them to me but they got mad because I spilled some water in one of them by accident. I was happy and didn't saw the bottle that one of the small ones had next to him. I kick it with my leg and the drawing got wet. I am not sure if mom kept that one too, but I like to think that it is still with the other drawings, saved in a box somewhere. I think I will look for them once we get back home. If it is still wet, I will try to fix it as much as I can.

Now, if only he would finish talking, let my mom go and take me back home with her, that would be very nice of him. That way I could be able to search for the drawings today. I know that the small ones with be happy too if I can fix the one I damaged by accident. They always are happy when I try to help them around the house. I may not be able to do much, but whatever I can do I do it as good as possible. And I know that they like that from me because they tell me that when I am done helping them out.

I don't think I remember the first time I saw them, and I don't know if they remember either. I can't tell how many times I have seen them leaving after I wake up, but I do remember one time when I went with them without mom. It was only once, but it was awesome.

The place was really big, and there were a lot of others walking around. That's what I noticed almost immediately: they all walked like them. Different than the way I walk. I saw a couple moving like me in the corner where a bigger one was helping others to cross the street but then they disappeared before I could go there too. One of the smaller ones touched me on my back, and then grabbed me by my stomach and raised me into a higher place, on top of a bench. I was not sure what I was supposed to do, so I just started saying the same things I always do when they come back home after lunch, but then another one placed two hands over my mouth. I guess they didn't want to hear me. I mean, it was not like they were coming back: they were already there with me! I stayed quiet and without moving. Then I saw the one that was helping the others coming in our direction. All of the small ones started to freak out and talked to each other in rapid succession. I couldn't understand what they were saying, and by the look of their faces, I tough that maybe we were in the same situation we were with mom when we shared food during lunch at home. Not a very good situation to be, honestly.

Mom came to the big place too sometime later and took me with her back home. She didn't say anything to me during the raid back, but I could tell that she was mad. I know the difference between good and bad, and her silent expression was telling me that I did something that she didn't like.

She opened the front door and helped me to get into the kitchen; then she brought something to eat for both, which was weird somehow. The sun was still low – I could see it thru the window from where I was sitting down – but I was a little hungry anyway and ate my meal without complaints. When I was done she took me to my bed and stayed with me until I fell asleep. I was really tired after that adventure! I was thinking already on doing it again and mom would probably be mad If I dared to do it. I guess there was only one way to know for sure.

The next morning, mom stayed by the kitchen door while the small ones were leaving again. I couldn't go with them since she was blocking my way out. She did the same thing for a few more days until I finally gave up on trying. I just stayed on my bed while watching them running outside. She allowed me to go to the porch after lunch to greet them and I was happy to do it every time, but in reality what I wanted to do was to go again with them, to that big place where I saw others like me.

I think she noticed my face when they were leaving one day after I wake up and didn't move from my bed without her telling me to stay inside. I think she noted that I didn't want to try again and probably felt bad about it because she gave me a little more food than the usual. I ate the whole plate without leaving my bed. There was no reason to stand up, after all. My legs were hurting a little, and I wanted to rest in bed for some more time.

She placed her hands on my back like she usually does every time I finish eating, and then she took me with her and we went outside. Fresh air is always nice after lunch, I think.

I thought we were just going to play outside, maybe in our porch or next to the bench. But she put me on her car and took me to a place that was very similar to where I went with the small ones, although not that big or scary. There were not that many like them around. The place was filled with others that walked exactly like me! She was smiling while we were going from one room to the other, and she allowed me to play with them. I never saw them before, and they probably never saw me either, but we started playing with each other almost immediately.

We stayed for a very long time in there and I was already losing all of my energy, but I wanted to stay for as long as possible. Mom went alone inside a different room for a couple of times and then she sat next to me while I was resting for a bit. I looked at her and she smiled. I bet she was happy as I was to be there too.

We went back home when the sun was getting very low again, and the dark was starting to cover everything around. The small ones were in the kitchen already eating and mom put me in my place and gave me my plate too. Maybe she wasn't that mad when I ate on my bed before. The small ones came and sat next to me with their plates and we started sharing our food again, and this time she didn't say anything to anybody. I guess the trip made her happy as it did to me. And I understand happy and sad pretty well.

I finished my meal, went to bed and fall asleep almost immediately. I didn't saw the small ones leaving the next morning, because they were gone by the time I woke up. Mom was eating by herself in silence, and she smiled when she saw me walking thru the kitchen door. She stood up and gave me water and then she went back to her chair and continued eating in silence. I sat next to her without saying a word until she was done. She walked to the porch and called me to go with her. That took me by surprise. Was she taking me to the same place we went to yesterday? I would not mind going again!

Sometime later, I was already playing with those that walk like me. There were some more than walk like mom – more than the day before – and they were all sitting together by the corner of the big yard, chatting and laughing. They all look happy to be there. And I was very cheerful too. We stayed for a very long time again and then went back home when the sun was getting low and the day was turning fresh and dark.

We did the same trip a lot of times, and it was always the same ones sitting by the corner while I and the others that walked like me were playing. Sometimes there were new faces, and there were others that I never saw again, but I was always overjoyed to play with them. The only problem was that my legs were hurting more and more every time we went back to that place; I always tried to forget about it, but I started to have a very hard time keeping up with the rhythm of the games.

I wasn't sure what was going on; mom didn't seem worried about it. She kept bringing me a lot of times and taking me back home when the sun was already very low. Something I didn't notice at first was that mom sometimes was not with the others by the corner for a very long time. But since she looked pleased while she was watching me and the others playing, I didn't take it as something important to worry about. If she needed to go somewhere else, I was fine as long as I was with the others. I was very happy, and I understand happy pretty well. I even forgot about that day when I was trying to greet the small ones closer to the street than the usual when they were coming back home after lunch, and something really big hit me without warning.

Mom made a face I never saw on her before when she went and checked on me. I couldn't walk or stand-up and she took me back home on her arms.

The small ones saw what happened and ran to where I was. They tried to help mom when she moved me but she was complaining to them that she was unable to walk with them on the way. Once we were inside she put me on my bed and I stayed there for the rest of the day until the sun was very low. She put a little something that looked like a rock on my mouth and then she told me to drink some water. The rock tasted weird and I wanted to spit it out but she put it back again. I tried again but she was quicker than me. I decided not to contradict her and swallowed the rock. She looked happy and walked to the kitchen to attend to the small ones. I think that she was still mad at them for trying to help her carrying me home because she told them not to sit with me on my side. I think she told them that because they stayed sitting afar from me and there was no other reason I could think of why they would not like to be with me.

My legs were hurting. I fell asleep and didn't notice if the small ones finally came and sit with me or not. I hope they did because I like that a lot.

III

Mom was directing her attention to him, but her hands were placed on my belly. I was still in the same place unable to move, and they were still discussing something that I couldn't understand. Her expression was a clear reflection of the pain I was feeling on my legs and my back. Her eyes were filled with water to the point of running droppings, like the flowers in the garden during the mornings after the days of cold. I'm sure she was in pain too, probably because of me. I mean, there was no other explanation. We were going to that place filled with others that walked like me for a very long time until I was unable to walk by myself. I remember one day when she took me to the porch and we stayed there for a longer time than usual. She talked to me very slowly and doing a lot of pauses, and then she took me to this place. And I didn't like it in here: the smell was really weird, and the sounds were scary. I couldn't move so I couldn't run back home, and the idea of not knowing what was happening around me was freaking me out like nothing else before today.

She nodded and the other one got closer to me. I saw again what I saw before on his hands but I didn't recognize what it was. I just felt a sting in one of my legs and then a hot sensation all around the lower part of my body. I noticed that the pain was starting to disappear, and I liked that a lot. Maybe I would be able to go back and play with the others that walk like me, or even better, go with the small ones again to that big place where they go after I wake up. I started to feel better just an instant after feeling the sting. This was awesome!

Mom was smiling while she was looking at me. I was sure she was feeling the same way I was feeling after the sting, but I didn't saw the other getting closer to her. Maybe she was just happy for me because the pain was going away and I was feeling better. Maybe she was also thinking about going to that place we went before so many times. Maybe she was missing the others that sat with her by the corner of the yard. She was always laughing when she was with them, so it was probably that.

She rubbed my belly in a very silly way but I like it, especially now that it was not hurting anymore when she touched me. I looked at her face with an expression like telling her to do it again, and I think she understood because she did it, several times, smiling and cleaning her eyes with her hands. The other got closer to her and said something to her ear, and I thought for a moment that she would be feeling the sting too; I saw her walking thru the door and going away. Is she leaving me here alone with the other? She was smiling at me and giving me silly belly rubs! She can't leave me now!

The sting was no longer hurting, but I was still feeling it somehow. Maybe this was supposed to happen. I was feeling great actually. Then mom came back and the small ones were with her. They were all smiling while they were looking at me. They got closer and made a circle around. The other was standing by the window, not that far away. It was like those days when we were all sitting at the kitchen after they came back home and we shared food from our plates, but they didn't have any food with them this time, as far as I could tell. Mom was talking to the other now, and the small ones were standing up around me. Maybe she was asking him to leave the room.

I was hungry, and I didn't want her to go out again. If the other was going to leave and bring something to eat for all of us, I wouldn't mind it at all.

But he stayed in the room with us, looking at each of the small ones smiling. Then mom got closer to him and told him something on his ear. She smiled too. Maybe everything was going to be Ok after all and all of my fears were unnecessary. But I still wanted to be sure that they were not going to leave me there, and still didn't want to be alone. I asked them to stay.

They started laughing after hearing me saying that, and I was not sure why. They got closer to me and gave me a big hug all at the same time. They were knocking their heads between each other trying to accommodate themselves in a circle, and they were laughing even more. Mom told them to go one by one and they did it as she said. The hugs were fantastic. I was feeling great now and tried to hug them back but I couldn't do it properly. They took my arms and placed them around their necks as if I was hugging them. I like that, and I think they liked it too.

The other got closer to me and put something in my chest. It was cold and hard. He then inserted something on his ears and nodded. One of the small ones grabbed him by his clothes and asked something. He removed the thing from his ears and put it in the ears of the small one. His eyes got bigger and her face was the same he did when I asked them to stay.

Another of the small ones asked too and all of them took turns and placed that thing on their ears. All of them opened their eyes to the maximum they could and made the same expression as the first one that tried that.

Mom was standing on the corner, watching them going again asking to use that on their ears. Maybe it was a new game that we never played before, but I was having a lot of fun just by looking at their faces. And I wasn't even moving. I liked this new game a lot.

IV

I don't know if the sting was supposed to do this, or if it was because the pain was no longer present and I was feeling great. I suddenly felt a desire to run outside rushing through my spine. I could feel the breeze already on my face, and the door was open. I tried to move a little and was unable to do it. My body simply didn't react. I tried again and was able to move one of my legs to the border of the bed. I tried one more time and moved the other leg too. One of the small ones saw what I was trying to do and started to cry. I didn't know this before. I never understood why they made that kind of noise while their face was all distorted when mom was mad at them for something they did, like pushing each other to the floor. But now I was fully understanding what the small one was doing. And it was probably because of me since I was unable to move my legs and my body and play with them.

As the pain was disappearing and I was feeling even better, I started to understand a lot of things I never understood before. Like why mom never wanted for me to go with them to that big place and why she took me instead to this other place: she wanted for me to be with others that walked like me. She wanted for me to spend time with them instead of being with the ones that walked like her. She was always taking care of me, even after that big and hard thing hit me when I got too close to the street. Now that I saw the little one crying because I was trying to run, I understood that she didn't want them to see me struggling to do very simple things. As I was getting worse with time, she probably thought that they would not be able to smile while I was deteriorating. She made a special ramp for me to be able to get on the bed when we all were taking a nap together and the small ones used it as a slide. It was a joy for them to play with it, and a bigger joy for me to watch them doing it. I wasn't even mad with them for using something that was supposed to be mine. I mean, we shared food every time we could; we could share this too for sure.

The pain was now gone; the sting was no longer there. The other was still talking to mom and the small ones were still in a circle. I wanted to tell them all that I was feeling great like never before and that I wanted to go home now. But my body was not reacting. Not a bit. Mom got closer and kissed me, then one by one the small ones started doing the same. A few moments later the big ones came to the room too and gave me big hugs. They were smiling but I could tell that they were trying hard to keep the smile on their faces. Something was not right. I couldn't say what, but seeing the big ones made me remember that they used to be small too, and they played with me a lot back then.

Seeing them as they were now, I suddenly realize that I saw them grow and became what they were now. They always took good care of me when mom was not around. Some of them were no longer living at home, but they came to visit from time to time. I started to wonder why they were here too.

Mom said something and everybody started to rub my belly as silly as she did before. And they all started to repeat something I heard them saying many, many times. Especially when we were playing outside while mom watched us, sitting at the porch and drinking from her cup.

When only mom and the others were in the room with me, I was unable to see them clearly and understand what they were saying and that got me scared for real. But now I was seeing everybody clear and I was understanding what they were saying. Maybe this was what the sting was supposed to do. Maybe because there was no more pain on me, I was finally able to understand. And I was feeling great.

One by one, they all started going to where the other was standing and gave him a hand, pretty much like how they give it to me when we meet for the first time, long time ago. I didn't remember this type of things before, but I was having old memories coming back to me in a very clear way. The sting was helping with that, I was sure! I remember when we went to the beach and played in the water until we all got dead-tired and sleep for hours in the sand. I remember when we were outside when the sun was down and *stayed* outside until it came back again, on the other side of the house.

We were playing with some objects that produced the same type of light that mom placed on the porch when she wanted to relax. We were again really tired after playing for so long.

I remember when I was with others that walk like me when I was small, and another mom came and took me with her. But we didn't go to her home. She took me directly to my mom, talked to her for a bit and she left. But I guess she didn't go that far away because I saw her several times after that, especially when I went outside to greet the small ones when they came home after lunch.

I remember that I always loved to play with the big ones when they were small. And when they got bigger, I loved to play with the others too.

Mom was always with us, watching and taking care while we were having the best time playing.

And I liked that a lot.

V

They were all talking at the same time and the words were getting mixed between each other. I was trying to tell them that I was understanding what they were saying to me over and over, but they were not listening. They were all laughing and giving me hugs and kisses, and silly belly rubs. They didn't stay quiet long enough for me to say something back. I screamed at them in an attempt to call for their attention and had no success at all. I rested my head back and stayed quiet instead.

The hot sensation that I was feeling on the lower section of my body expanded into the higher parts. I remember that this place was cold when we got here, but not anymore. It was now feeling like being outside after lunch. Mom called everybody to a corner and they all got there in silence. The other went with them too. I may be able to tell them now what I wanted to say before! I started by telling them that I was feeling like new and that we could go back home if they wanted it too. I also said that I was seeing clearly and that I was understanding a lot of things I never understood before. I was remembering a lot of events, like the time when we played in the rain and mom got *really, really* mad with everybody for the mess we did in the living room. Or the other time when we all stayed outside for the whole night in the middle of a forest, eating sweet things while sitting next to a fire. I was now understanding a lot of things about them and especially about myself. I continue telling them all that and more, but they were just looking at me and started laughing. It was a good laugh though, like the one they did when we all saw the ocean together for the first time.

I tried to stand up once more, but again my body refused to move. Only my legs were shaking a little; mom came over and touched them while she bends over and places her face directly in front of mine. Then the other came over too. I saw my image reflected on mom's eyes. The big ones got closer to me, while the small ones stayed by the corner, watching. There was no pain, but I couldn't move at all. Mom gave me another kiss and called the small ones. They made a bigger circle this time.

The sting I felt before was something good. The hot sensation that covered all of my body started to dissipate, slowly at first. The room was feeling a little chill now. I tried once more to tell them, but I could see that they didn't understand. They were in silence and they heard me well, but they couldn't make sense of my voice. I feel bad for not being able to tell them what I wanted to say, now that I was understanding what they were telling me all the time.

There was nothing else to do. They were here with me at this special moment, hugging me and giving me the best and silly belly rubs I ever had, and that was all that matters. For them, for me and of course, for mom. What else could I ask from them, anyway?

I was feeling sleepy now, and my eyes felt like they had some weight attached to them. The other was working on some screens and pressing buttons, and the noise in the room was reduced to almost nothing.

Only the small ones were making the same noise that one of them did when I tried to move before. But I am not mad at them, not anymore. They can do that if they like it. I am happy for them.

I stayed quiet for some time, looking at them, smiling. They smiled back, or at least that's what I think they did. I was losing my vision again, but this time I didn't care. I just wanted to sleep. They did all they could do for me. Especially mom. I understood that now.

After all, and as I was supposed to respond to them when they asked this to me every time while we were playing together outside under the sun, I am…

No, I *was* always a good boy".

Twenty-Five

I

He has been waiting for the coffee to be ready, smelling the aroma that invades the whole house and invites to sit at the table to strike a conversation. Any topic would do it, as long as there are dynamics on the talking and no phone screen checking allowed. Just talk; maybe about the eternally postponed family vacation at the beach, or the long-awaited time for retirement, now closer than he ever wanted it to be. Today the entire house is amazingly quiet, all for himself at the moment. Not a single voice or sound and not a soul around. He can hear all the noises coming from outside and all the cracks and screams created by the house as it rocks with the wind. He recalls very well all those hectic days when chats were coming from the TV set on the living room, steps coming down from the stairs and walking on the upper level that can resonate below. Today he can even hear the fridge singing a very interesting melody while it makes ice and drops it on the collector below the machine that forms the little cubes continuously and without interruptions.

It's not going to be like this forever of course. She will be back pretty soon. In the meantime, he goes to the cabinet next to the fridge and picks a spoon from under some of the discount coupons he stores in the drawer after removing them from the coffee cans. His favorite flavor from his preferred maker at a reduced price? always a great idea to have them around, just in case. *"I'm sure I am not the only one! –* he always tries to explain himself when he places a new one in the drawer, much to her disbelief.

The school buses passed by, one after the other, and the last one made a stop to pick up the neighbor's kids but nobody ran out from this home to catch it. At least not anymore. He remembers so darn well the morning rush, the noise and the last minute questions from his kids about where they left their homework last night – it was always laying spread across the small central table in the living room, in front of the TV -, where their favorite hoodie that never gets washed was or why the waffles were still cold to the touch although that never stopped them from finish the entire box in a blip. He can almost see them all again in front of him having breakfast or running to catch the bus while he waves them goodbye from the front porch. He remembers those hectic mornings, filled with the same aroma that now reminds him to take the good old and rusty metallic coffee mug from the side table and get himself a healthy dose of "wake-me-up" in liquid form.

He's been watching the same buses coming and going every morning for the last few years after everybody left home for good; some to start a family of their own and some because they simply wanted out to demonstrate that they could go without any more help from them. One can't simply stop their desire for independence once their minds are all set on going away.

He's been remembering those mornings running thru all the same details every time, trying to keep the memories from fading away – which has proven to be more difficult with every passing day – ratifying the simple fact in life that age and memory loss go hand by hand. Or at least that's what the good Doctor told him when he went for his annual checkup a couple of weeks ago. He's been feeling the blues recently as he thinks about all the adventures they have shared, good and bad and all the discussions around her jumps, even that those have been placed on hold for a very long time now.

"It's been a very good stretch without them" – he thinks as he sips some coffee, smiling with satisfaction after feeling the same glorious sensation on his throat that he feels every time, every morning.

She finally came back from outside with a heap of papers and envelopes of all shapes and colors and placed them next to the peanut butter jar by the dinner table. He doesn't care about that colorful stack anyway; his eyes are glued to the last one still on her hands. She seems genuinely worried, with a dark shadow on her eyes and an absence of color from her cheeks. This is his biggest concern: to not disrupt her edginess even more than he has done already. But this is not one of those times when he can do something about. He offers comfort and support by taking her hand and grabbing the envelope from it, while guides her to take a seat at the living room. He grabs his cup of coffee at the last second, and she smirks at him with an understanding nod of her head.

Once they are sitting down on the big couch, they look at each other for a very long time like they have done it a thousand times before when there was something important to discuss between them. They both tried to smile almost at the same time while taking a deep breath before opening the envelope and reading the letter that was inside.

The coffee was tasting especially good today, precisely when he needed reassurance about something as complicated as life, or simple and mundane as his daily morning ritual at the kitchen table, with her by his side.

II

White everywhere. That's what's keeping him distracted the whole time. There is almost no color around the room, with exception of the TV set, high in the wall and turned to the local news, and all of the screens in every machine connected to his body. Even the curtains that cover the window to his left are of a pale tone of gray that can pass for a delicate tone of white if you didn't pay enough attention to it. Color is what he misses the most. Color and the aroma of real coffee brewing in his stove.

Now is not the time for memories of fading ghosts running around the house or sitting in front of him at the kitchen table while they check the latest post from friends and foes, and he knows that very well. Now is the time for planning and preparation, awkward conversations and to listen to the never-ending stories from when he was young, stupid and wild coming from his friends and long lost acquaintances from work, the local bar at the north corner of the Square downtown or some other places he doesn't even remember that well, but that suddenly are coming back from his past. All of them are well intended, of course. All of them trying to keep their composure and look like nothing really important is happening around and right in front of their eyes. Their body language does the talk for them, and he grows worried about giving them a hard time just by being there.

She's not with him this morning; she's been busy talking with the administrators and personnel attending their case, and that has been taking a lot of time and coordination for both. At first, he gets anxious about her absence but then remembers the conversation they had a few nights ago. She insisted on talking about what he wanted to do in the next few days, and how he wanted to spend their time in between. They talked about trips and home projects planned a long time ago, charity work at their local Church and maybe – just maybe – offering their help at the City's Summer Carnival just to bail out at the last minute like they did every year just for the adrenaline rush they got while fielding the calls they would receive for sure. It was almost like a sport for them.

They talked that night until the sunrise was showing up at the window without even feeling tired or sleepy, which was satisfactory and unnatural at the same time. She was uneasy, but he kept reassuring her that his plan was as good as any other plan they talked about already. It will not take her much time of effort – or at least that was what he thought – and she would not even need to leave the hospital to take care of his desire. And if there was something she wanted to do right now was precise to attend to his requests. She thought that, after all the events that had passed for them in the past weeks, and especially after so many times he was there for her, he had earned the right to ask for this favor without questions from her part. Now, on the other hand, the *special request* he made with a pamphlet full of vibrant colors and catching phrases included during his "presentation", was a different story to digest. It took her by surprise when he mentioned that to her for the very first time, and still surprised her every time he went back to the same conversation about it. There would be time to revisit this topic with him if she ever crossed over her self-imposed barrier of credibility about it.

It was not that crazy of an idea, but it was simply something she never thought about. She wasn't even sure if that option existed in the area, but based on the information on the pamphlet – and all of the research already made by him, extremely extensive and detailed to the point of obsession – it was an attainable reality for them.

She came back to his room while the nurse was leaving after changing the needles and the bags with fluids, and checking the charts for the thousandth time today. She noticed his expression of concern and the question marks floating on his eyes. That was the same expression he had since the day they sat and had the talk while drinking cold tea at their porch. She smirks and gave him a little nod, almost imperceptible for the untrained eye. After living together for so many years, they had developed their own way to communicate with the less amount of words or gestures. A simple movement of her head was enough for him to bring back the widest smile on his face, some color to his cheeks and a worried look from the nurse, who noticed the change in his mood right away.

He was so happy now, that he didn't pay attention to the crumpled piece of paper in her hand, or the pencil balancing on her ear. She was back and he needed to know the news for sure as preparation to start the next step on his plan. There was so much to do and the idea of actually doing it was enough of a pinch that he almost stood up to hug her. The IV running from the post to his arm was a friendly reminder to stay put and wait until she came close to him instead.

He just wanted to see the list with all the names checked out, and the date set by both confirmed with a big and imperfect circle around it.

She sat down for a moment at one of those lounge chairs with long leg supports that were placed all around in the main lobby area, down on the first floor. She needed to put her thoughts in order and clarify her mind before going to the phone booths to start with the calls she had scheduled for today. Why did they never purchase a piece of furniture like this for their home? It was ridiculously cozy and gentile with her back and feet. She recalled their first living room set they found at the local flea market and that was carried away by a friend. It was nice and cheap and served them well for many years until they donate it to charity, freshly cleaned and reupholstered by a professional.

The first reflection that came to her mind after a few minutes of solitude in the chair was a very simple inquiry that has been doing rounds on her mind for a while by now. And although she knew she was not ready to receive a response from anybody – and especially not from herself-, she was still amazed by the sound of those words on her brain.

'Why him and not me?"

There was a certain level of envy on her reproach. But this was not a consequence of feeling pain for having him hosted in that room, even that her soul was aching more with every passing day. It was rather the curious combination of the outcome from multiple tests runs under the concept of seeking the checkered flag at the end of a run, and the effect of her genuine aspiration to finally meet her designated Valkyrie for once. There was no rush, of course, but the desire was by all accounts in there permanently, embedded in everything she did and said, although hiding almost all the time. This was not one of those times.

She wasn't happy with the way her path was bending lately, but her despondency was a long-stored concept for the two of them. And this was not the time to bring the idea afloat all over again. She was struggling to keep up with the demands of the occasion, and with her genuine impulse to provide support and comfort to him, who needed it the most. It was a battle against time, and even that she was in total control of it during her enduring fight with her own demons, it was now something out of her hands. It was clear what she needed to do and how she needed to do it. But it was also something that appeared harder than expected, especially under the circumstances of their past. Why was she having such a hard time putting aside her struggle and simply focus her attention on him this time? He was needing her, and she was not going anywhere, other to the phone booths area to make some calls.

She had a lovely task on hand, and her feathers felt the wind commanding them to move as it did in the past. Only if she could raise from that damned comfy chair.

She went thru all the names on the list, and the order she needed to place before deciding that it was time to stand up. Her feet felt like human feet again and her back was in one piece, well-rested and ready to go. She looked inside her bag and noticed that she forgot a key element back home, right on top of the spoons. She would need to go back and return on time before they could do anything else about the rest of their plan.

The music at the lobby was inviting, and the chaos of the last weeks was a friendly reminder to her to stay a little longer sitting in there, but there was a lot to do and she would need to do it by herself this time. It was not that she was incapable of doing it, but she was used to having him with her while running errands, if not helping at least keeping her company and talking about nothing in particular. Now she would need to adapt again to the circumstances. Fortunately for both, he was always very cautious with anything related to legal matters. All of the paperwork was ready and signed by him, and she would need to just follow up and ask for dates and locations. Even for that little project of him.

That thought made her smile and recoil from where her mind was wandering without control while drifting downstream, too close to the rapids. It was time to shake the negativity from her brain, to clean the dust from her wings and to finally stand up from the couch. There was a lot of people depending on her, and a lot of activities that will require her full attention in the days to come. Was she even ready for that?

There was only one way to find about it, she thought as she reluctantly stood up at once and started walking away from the area, turning her head around every few steps and thinking on going back for a little more.

The list was not that long, and most of the lines were already crossed out. Those still pending would need to wait for later. She was back on his room and was telling him how they were doing so far. He had a special spark on his eyes as he was listening to her going thru all the names, one by one. He was making a lot of questions and this was irritating her a lot. Why was he so impatient? Why now? There was still time, and the plan was getting along pretty well.

But she knew him, and she understood his worried words almost immediately after feeling irritated for a brief moment. It was not him making her feeling mad; it was her own struggle to stay calm and focused on what was causing her anger to get afloat. She would need a little more effort and energy than what she anticipated, after all.

She was a fighter. This was nothing compared with some episodes from her past. It was just a matter to take action and convince herself, again, that there was no need to jump never more.

IV

Noises of conversation in every tone imaginable can be heard from far away in the long corridor, from the elevators to the bathroom stalls at the other side; all coming from one single room by the left side, almost in front of the nurse's station. Male and female, young and old; baritone, soprano and something in between. All talking at the same time, all of them laughing to the same old jokes. All around him barely fitting in the reduced space, limited even more with the extra chairs placed one next to the other while he is trying to keep his posture in a way that the needles do not hurt that much this time. All of them eating from their own plates, although the youngest ones were trying to share their meals or exchange some items they didn't like for some other closer to their taste. The floor was starting to get covered with the remains of the struggle they had while keeping their plates on their laps.

Fresh coffee and pancakes are a staple item given the time of the day, but there is also plenty of fruit, cereal, yogurt and some boxes with candy, comfitures and even a few plates with home-made chocolate chip cookies that somebody brought from the restaurant in the first floor, probably without permission from the doctor in charge.

But nobody was thinking or worrying about it, at least not today.

This was a day to enjoy the company of each other, the food and the aroma surrounding the area that could wake up somebody from a coma. The nurses turned their heads away and made it like they didn't even notice – with a grin on their faces. The extra cookies and cups of fruit placed next to their phone station was a very good help with their acceptance of the event, of course.

She's been standing next to him the whole time, helping him while he was enjoying a freshly brewed cup of coffee like he used to do it every morning, back at home. He's weak now and needs some help holding the cup, but the spirit in that room made him feel like the strongest man on Earth. He could barely hold his arms up to drink, but she was quick to take his hands in between hers and then passed him a disposable towel to clean his mouth. He smiles at her, and she knew exactly what he was meaning with that devilish smile: he wants a kiss from her, but not in front of the kids. Maybe later. She knows very well they would not mind at all and would probably have a blast and a lot of laughs if they see them kissing, but gladly accepts to wait. There will be time for that later on.

The Doctor comes back with some papers and the latest results on his hands, but he stops cold at the door watching the scene that's happening in there. He hesitates for a few seconds, nodes at them and turns around, leaving them with their party but not without first accepting an offering of scrambled eggs and fried bacon strips on a toasted bun that somebody left untouched, and a cup of black coffee that made his eyes roll in satisfaction.

His stomach reminds him very loudly that the apple slices and the bottle of water at his desk are in no way a proper replacement for this meal from heaven. He walks away without saying anything else, but just some barely perceptible "thanks" to her while placing his hand on her shoulder as he approaches the door. She nods and smiles back to him in response, but her expression says it all. He knows she's getting worried about the toll this party is taking on him, and that he may need some extra sleep just to stay strong for the medication he's now taking via the IV on his arms. He knows he will need to keep an extra eye on the machines connected to him, just in case.

He walks out of the room and goes to the nurse's station to write some additional instructions on their diary and takes a couple of cookies from their plate. They are not happy about this, and he notes it on their faces while he walks away, biting one of the cookies as he goes in direction to his office, situated on the same floor.

She keeps helping him with everything as she wants him to truly enjoy every moment as it passes. The noise in the room is now noticeably higher than it would be considered accepted or even permitted in the building, but nobody has come to complain so far. It seems like everybody agreed that morning, to let them have their party in peace.

There was no music of course, but the sound of all their voices talking at the same time got a rhythm and cadence by its own. She looks around with satisfaction, noticing the void that was making its rounds on her before was nowhere to be felt.

She's good now, knowing what this means to him. His expression as he talks to everyone in the room is a vivid reminder of the times they have spent together, since the day he knocked twice at her door with the bouquet of roses. It has been a wild ride for both.

Their laughs grow stronger as he starts talking about the time when they meet, thinking how beautiful she was. She reaches and gives him a little pat on his shoulder, and he corrects himself and says how beautiful *she is*. Everybody starts collecting their used plates and the chairs, as he calls her with a very simple gesture of his hand. She takes a small towel from the side of the bed and cleans his face carefully as he looks directly on her eyes.

He's about to say something but she interrupts him by placing her index finger in front of his mouth.

"Yeah, I know. Me too."

V

She's by the elevators taking care of the last ones leaving the Hospital, saying thanks to the adults and kissing goodbye to the kids, while hugging them all one by one. It's hard to let them go and the hugs are stronger and last longer every time. It's has been a very hectic week and everybody is coming to terms in their own way. There is no rush, no questions about lost homework or misplaced unwashed hoodies. There is no school bus making a stop by the front gate or coffee brewing and engulfing the room with an aroma that can wake up a drunken youngster from his sleep, after partying the night before. The long hallway from the elevators to the bathroom is quiet now, and the nurses are busy trying to figure out who is next on their rounds. She gives the last kisses and hugs and returns to his room in silence, walking almost without thinking where she is going.

The color is absent again from the space, except for the TV, hanging high on the wall, tuned to the local news. This time the screen on every machine is turned off and the silence is deafening. She knows that this is normal after all that happened the night before. She tries to tidy up the room a little, very accustomed to a daily routine that engulfed her whole universe for a few weeks. She stops and reflects on what she is doing, turns back and sits on a chair next to his bed for a few minutes. She takes his hand on hers and remembers the list that she prepared with his help that night at the porch when they were making plans. She takes the crumpled piece of paper from her purse and checks again for every name, every phone number and every meal plate for the order she needed to place at the dinner located on the first floor of the Hospital: 7 adult plates with scrambled eggs and bacon in a toasted bun, fruit and orange juice on the side; 5 extra plates for every plus-one but adding cereal and yogurt on each of them in case their youngsters wanted to explore; 9 kid's plates that include pancakes with a happy face made of wiped cream and chocolate chips, fruit and orange juice in a bottle. Two plates of salad and vegan wrap for the ones who decided that the old man's way of living was not good enough for them. She smiles while re-checking this last two items off of her list and remembers so many discussions about food, exercise and even books to read, with him giving them hell for the decisions they made. She smiles because she remembers how he lost those heated arguments every single time.

Two more plates on her list had to be specially made by the kitchen staff, after her explaining the reasons behind the strange request for additions to the eggs and bacon in a bun, in one of them: freshly brewed coffee made with a very specific brand and served in a rusty old metallic cup; home-made-looking chocolate chip cookies on two styles: chewy and crunchy; a peanut butter jar and toast, and a little toy for every kid in the family, packed individually in a small gift bag with a cartoon character in the front but placed all together in a big brown bag with no marks at all on the outside. She knows they will love to receive that toy from him, and she knows he will love it, even more, giving them something to play with.

She looks at the names, all crossed from the list. All called in. All accounted for. A helper from the kitchen is now picking up the dirty dishes and trash and she stands up from the chair to help. She has never been one to stay on the side without doing anything if something needs to be done. Besides, keeping herself busy would help her with thinking calmly about the completion of his final wishes, now that all the paperwork is done.

Carefully, she places the old and rusty coffee cup back in the little box where it was before. She will need to think very carefully where this particular item will be placed for good.

Three Hundred and Fifty

For her, this was home. Maybe not in the normal sense of the word, but for all practical reasons, it was. She even had a beautiful hand-made quilt fully spread across her bed, with a red ribbon making waves around the edge. It was a Christmas' present given by her mother a long time ago, created with pieces of shirts, jeans and lots more of multicolored cloths. A truly treasured possession proudly displayed for anyone who wanted to hear the story behind it.

A rocking chair with a cozy pillow was placed by the window, and a black floor fan was making smooth passes with almost no sound from a corner, pushing a fresh breeze across the room. The TV set was tuned to the local news, although the volume was set to a barely perceptible level. There was a lot of greeting cards hanging from cork panels at the left side of the door, going from side to side across the entire wall. One could check the dates and would find that they were from several months back, up until a couple of days ago. They didn't have a specific topic or theme but rather they include almost any imaginable type of figures and designs. Lots of them had handwritten notes that were made clearly by kids, and some were simply signed at the bottom of the imprinted message inside. But they all shared a common denominator, bright and colored, placed on the top right corner of their covers.

She was resting her feet inside one of those massaging machines that circulate hot water with a little pump - way noisier than the floor fan – while sitting on the edge of her bed. She was looking to the outside with her eyes lost in the horizon. Hers was one of the best rooms in the Adult Care wing at the Hospital: being a senior resident seems to have some privileges after all. Her window was facing a small park full of trees and benches, and lots of people running or walking in exercise clothing. Most of that people were nurses and doctors from the same building where she was, either getting ready to come over for work or already out from their shifts. There were also tenants from the apartment complex that surrounded the area. She fell envy every time she saw those people outside, not because she was unable to go there with them, but because she would be unable to keep up with their pace.

A nurse walked inside just enough to say Hi to her, and she answered with a smile. Everybody knew her. There was always somebody to chat and share stories with. She had a very unique talent to keep a group entertained for a very long time, and she was happy to comply if they asked for her company. It was always a nice relaxed moment for both parties, especially after a very busy day. Her feet were no longer the same, but that little pump was doing wonders with the little bubbles of hot water that were dancing around her toes.

She took her feet out of the water and started drying them with an embroiled towel. Another Christmas gift, probably. She then laid down on her bed and worked the TV remote to pump the volume up a little more, just in time to catch the start of her favorite show.

Another nurse came to the room with a note on her hand and placed it on the nightstand that was closer to the door, next to an old analog alarm clock and a black rotary phone. Both of those items looked out of place next to the machines that were standing firm behind the door, but she was a woman of traditions and a very clear and defined opinion about what she wanted around her, for all that one could tell. The note was supposed to stay there for the entire night as was the case most of the times, but a little detail included on it got her attention and made her stand up enough to grab it and read it. An almost childish smirk appeared on her face, and a little giggle was perceptible enough for the nurses on the station outside her room to try to peek inside and see what was going on. They would have to wait until the next morning to know.

She bent over to the right side of the bed and opened the top drawer of the little cabinet that was located there. She took a black notebook and a pen and started making some notes on it. She put both objects back where they were before and opened the lower drawer, extracting a small index card box from the back of it. Carefully she started going thru the multitude of cards inside of the box until she found one in particular that looked like some kid had been playing with it for some time. It was filled with dark spots, dirty splash of some kind of liquid and had two corners missing. She read it a couple of times and then placed it in the same spot where the nurse had left the note on the other side of her bed. She put the index card box back on the lower drawer and took the black notebook out again to review some other notes from a couple of days before. She needed to be sure she would have everything she will be needing.

As she started thinking about the request, she remembered where the closest store that carried that particular blend was located, all across the park with the lake. It was a beautiful walk, but a little far away for her tired feet.

"I guess the little bubbles machine will need to work overtime when I come back" – she thought as she placed the notebook back on the drawer and turned her night light off, getting ready to sleep – *"I thought I was the only one with that preference in particular, but I guess there are more crazy people around that I ever imagined"*.

II

The daily routine was always the same: dishes ordered by the resident nutritionist with very specific instructions on how to prepare and serve them. One piece of paper for every patient, protected inside a plastic cover to use them more than once. The staff was very used to follow these indications to the letter, knowing by a fact that an error on their part could have severe repercussions in the health of somebody else. They took their job very seriously and with pride, and they were always looking for each other, not as a team but more like a family filled with rules and traditions.

She was walking around the first floor trying to clear her mind when the aroma of freshly made food made her turn the corner to the left instead of turning right. Following what she thought was smelling like Canadian bacon she found the dinner by the end of the corridor. This was familiar territory, as she had worked in several kitchens thru the years. Nobody said anything when she walked inside and started looking at the frantic scene that was happening in front of her eyes, with a lot of people moving around and in between multiple industrial-grade stoves and ovens. Only a delivery boy that was placing bags of frozen vegetables in a gigantic walk-in fridge moved towards her and asked if she was lost or if she was looking for somebody. His comment was received with a smile and not a forced one.

A sincere gesture. He could see the light reflecting on her eyes for a couple of seconds before she went back to her thoughts. It was like throwing a rock at a pond and watch it skipping the water briefly before sinking to the bottom for good.

She didn't say anything back to him. He walked away and continued unloading some more boxes of groceries in silence.

One of the cooks noticed her standing next to the cutting table and pointed to the sink while keep looking at her. He made a gesture mimicking the act of washing his hands. She understood, walked to the sink and started washing hers. He pointed to his apron and then to one box placed in a shelf at her side. She nodded, grabbed the box and placed it on the table. There were aprons, hairnets, gloves, shoe covers, all nicely packed inside. She took a complete kit and got ready in minutes. He then moved his hands gesturing her to get closer. She started walking towards him but then circled back and walked to the same sink instead, washed her hands again and pointed to the box. He responded with the widest smile she could ever see before. She knew perfectly well that he understood what she just did, and he was visibly happy about it. She then approached him and stayed to his side for the rest of the day, observing and asking a lot of questions about what they were doing, the instructions on the papers and their tools inventory. She was deeply interested in how the place was managed, and the rules that everybody needs to follow. He was more than happy to explain everything to her with patience, although he needed to move around constantly and his explanations were given in paused moments between taking big pots from the fire, cutting enormous amounts of fruit and bagging a lot of individual slices of bread. She was not allowed to touch anything, but nobody said she couldn't stay there as much as she pleased. And she stayed until her feet started to hurt for being standing up on the same spot for so long.

For the first few days, she spent most of the time just watching and learning, trying to memorize the names and roles of everybody and helping to place the trays on the delivery carts, making sure that the instruction papers were perfectly visible with the patient's name to the front. This was a place of non-stop action, and she was always walking from one point to the other. There was little time to rest, but the satisfaction of routinely doing something like this was a real catharsis for her. It has been a very long time since she was working in a place like this, but her memory was coming back and her abilities appeared like they never went away. Years of practice were showing quick, and everybody noticed that almost immediately. Soon she was constantly asked for help at every work station around, and she was really happy to take part in all of that.

She was only worried about her Doctor's opinion after the latest event, but he gave her the green light once he saw her in action, per request of the Chief of Staff.

She was in her element and one could tell just by looking at her face. The Doctor was extremely surprised by the level of energy that she was demonstrating while she was helping everybody and moving around like nothing. The only indication for her was to take enough breaks and to make sure to take the prescribed pills for her condition.

The delivery boy brought a big whiteboard during one of his rounds and they placed it by the pantry, where they all could check the times and doses and they were all making sure she was alright at all times. One of the helpers made a special corner for her where she could take a breath and give her feet some time to recover. They wanted her around, but they couldn't afford to leave their stations if they need to take care of her if something happened all of a sudden.

A family with rules, indeed.

III

It was not an uncommon request, but it was usually prepared for kids at the Cancer Research Center or during Holidays for the Hospital Staff; never for a specific patient. But the idea was already living and breathing on her mind since she read the note the night before and especially after noticing the extra detail accompanying it. She knew the perfect recipe, but she had to order a few items that were missing from the pantry. There was still time, and apparently, money was not an issue. Whoever wrote the note was truly clear with the indications, and included a check for a particularly generous amount, well over what it was needed.

She was reading the note again when the delivery boy arrived by the back entrance. He was pulling a dolly with a few boxes, and he took the one on the top and placed it at the table, in front of her.

She started taking the items out and placing them side by side while checking them out from the list. He noticed an item that was already crossed, and he was about to ask her why when she turned around an opened a cabinet that was on top of the small sink behind her. That was her personal cabinet, and nobody messed with her or the contents on it. She took a big red can topped with a brown thick plastic lid and placed it with the rest of the groceries. The boy was curious and took it for a moment to read the label, but her glance was enough of a deterrent for him and put it back with a quick movement. The can almost felt from the table, but she grabbed it on time with a quick movement and put it back where it was before.

He did recognize the brand and understood why she crossed it from the list before giving it to him in the morning. He was also intrigued on why she needed it, given that they had an entire section in the pantry with a multitude of brands and flavors, but he learned long time ago not to ask her about her intentions when she was preparing special meals by request. She was always the one that everybody approached for things like this, and the kitchen staff was cool with that. It gave her great satisfaction to know that somebody enjoyed something especially prepared by her.

He was interested to know if they did have that particular brand on hand, but decided that right now was not the proper time to check. He would come back later, just to satisfy his curiosity.

This time, she asked for help pretty much like when they needed to work out a special order for a holiday or a birthday party, although on a smaller scale. It was not about the amount of work needed but rather about putting all of her attention into two specific items on the list. Two young apprentices accepted the challenge and started working their way around the preparations for the main entrees and side dishes. She was quick to point out any missing component or errors, and they responded with just a smile and a shrug of their shoulders, following her indications to the letter. She finished giving them the last instructions and placed a small saucepan on the stove to melt some butter. One of the apprentices noted that she was using the unsalted type; the other wrote down a quick note about it in a little notebook that he kept on his apron all the time.

She went to the tools cabinet and came back with a big mixing bowl, three large baking sheets, and an equally large pair of cooling racks. The butter was ready after waiting for a few minutes and she mixed it with the rest of the ingredients without any kind of rush on her movements. Using a tablespoon, she started scooping small balls and placed them on one of the cookie sheets, almost touching one to each other. The same apprentice that took note before asked her why she didn't leave any spacing between the little balls, and she simply looked at him while she finished covering the whole surface with more balls, took that sheet full to the edges and walked towards the walk-in fridge. She opened the door and went inside, coming back with empty hands. She smiled like a little kid as she was passing by, hitting her hands between them to get rid of all the loose flour right in front of him.

He took another quick note on his little notebook, now about chilling the dough balls before baking. The other assistant was working on the side dishes and main courses for the kids but he saw the whole episode and was unable to contain a laugh after seeing her reaction to the questioning by his friend. She was still standing close to them and saw how the second assistant was laughing almost in silence but in an extremely noticeable way. She walked to the table where she mixed the dried ingredients, rubbed her hands on the remaining flour and went back to the side dishes table. She repeated the same expression and hand movement as before while keeping her eyes fixed on the still laughing boy. A white cloud stayed hanging in front of him for a few seconds. Now the three of them were laughing at unison.

She was mean most of the time, but everybody knew the kind of sense of humor she had and that her mean attitude was only a tool on the arsenal that she uses to keep control during the food preparations. Mostly with young employees.

Especially with young and new employees.

IV

Once all three baking sheets were on the fridge, she cleaned the table and placed the bowl on the big sink, removed her apron, head-cover and gloves and took a sit on a rocking chair that looked exactly like the one she had on her room, placed on the little corner that was made for her almost since she started helping around. There was nothing else to do for at least a couple of hours before continuing with the next step, and she needed to rest for a little bit. Her feet were complaining all morning today, but they would have to wait until the order was finished, packed and delivered upstairs.

The young apprentices started cleaning the tools and moving the remaining items around the table to make some room for the individual trays. Even that they still had plenty of time to start the actual food preparation, they wanted to measure how much space they would need on the delivery cart. One of them continued bringing the rest of the ingredients from the pantry while the other removed all his cooking clothes and walked towards the back entrance. As he was passing in front of her, she took a little note from a small side table and gave it to him. It had a number written on it. He looked at it and gave it back to her. His nodding was a clear signal that he knew where that room was located. He waved his hand to his friend and walked out.

A couple of hours later, the oven was already set to the required temperature and she was humming a song while placing the dough balls – now with the proper separation between them – again on the baking sheets.

The apprentices were busy finishing the rest of the dishes and placing them on individual trays, with thermos covers on top to keep them hot. The first delivery cart was full and another took its place. Now it was the turn for the cold dishes and sides. They noticed the song that she was humming, but since none of them was unable to recognize, they assumed that it was an oldie and didn't follow up with her. They had a radio there, but she was always turning it off when they tried to listen to some of their favorite tunes. After a few failed attempts to convince her, they decided to simply listen to her humming instead.

She took the first batch of freshly baked cookies and left them on the baking sheet for a few more minutes, to give them a chewy consistency before placing them on the cooling rack. She did the same with at least half of the rest while moving the other half immediately from the cooking sheet and into the cooling rack until they were all done. The delivery carts were already aligned next to the door for the service elevator and a big unmarked bag full of toys was on the table. She inspected everything twice and then went to the stove for the last item on the list. She took a big black thermos from the small sink under her cabinet and filled it with a very aromatic beverage. The smell of cookies and brewed coffee made the rest of the staff at the kitchen to stop for a few seconds and turn their heads towards her. She smiled back in a way that was easily interpreted by them as a promise to do the same for the entire crew, some other day.

She grabbed the box that was brought earlier by one of the apprentices and took a rustic old metallic cup from it. She looked at it for a few seconds, trying to imagine the stories behind it or the significance that it may have to the recipient of the special meal. She was old school – as attested by the items that made her room's décor - and was aware of how an old object like this could become invaluable with time. Her first assumption was that this probably was an old gift by somebody important on the owner's life, like a mom or a dad, or maybe one of the sons or daughters. Her second guess was that maybe the owner was simply too cheap to buy a new one given that this was still in good shape. She placed it upside down on the last tray and closed the car's door. The apprentices started rolling them out of view towards the exit.

She went back to her cabinet on top of the little sink and grabbed a coffee mug, old and metallic, with black dots where the paint was chipped away with the use. It was funny to think that somebody else could be as cheap as she was, and kept an old cup as it was the case with hers. She poured some coffee on it and took a long sip. She grabbed the big red can – now without the brown plastic tap on it – and noticed that it was almost empty.

The walk to that old mom-and-pop grocery store that has this brand was a long one, but as she thought before when she noticed the little coupon attached to the note, the long walk to buy another one – this time for her - was worth it.

"Good coffee at a discounted price and very good service. You can't go wrong with that".

V

There was a plate on the table with five cookies on it. She took one and covered the others for when the young apprentices were back. She walked to the corner and took a sit on the rocking chair, still with the cookie on one hand and the coffee mug on the other. She took a bite and then a sip and rested her head on the high back support of the chair while starting rocking back and forth. The aroma was still lingering around and the noise was now back to normal-crazy for the hour. She was still thinking and wondering why they choose that brand, but she got herself a response after the second sip. The store that had it was a few blocks away and across the Main Park, but she never complained about it. The park was filled with trees and there was a little lake in the middle, under a lovely bridge. She usually made this trip only once a month, but it seemed like it was that time already.

The apprentices were back a few minutes later with the delivery carts empty. They both took a seat next to her but not without first grabbing one cookie each from the covered plate, per her indication. They looked at her for a couple of seconds, like little kids that just got back from school and were enjoying a snack with their mom. She nodded at them and smiled with satisfaction. One more special delivery complete.

She took another bite and a sip of her coffee, and they took a bite to the cookies on their hands. They all left a long sigh of satisfaction, clearly audible across the room. All of a sudden, she stands up and walks back to the cabinet on top of the little sink, grabs a plastic box from inside and removes the cover. She looks carefully until she finds what she was looking for and extract a small piece of paper, carefully putting it on her purse. She goes back to the chair and continues enjoying her coffee. The two apprentices looked at her but said nothing about it. But she knows them very well and realizes they must be intrigued.

"There is no good on going to the store for another can if I don't have a coupon with me for it. Good coffee, with a killer discount, included in the price. They don't make it like that anymore" – The apprentices nod in silence, and take another bite to their cookies almost at the same time. She laughs at them thinking how much they will need to learn if they want to be taken seriously by anybody else outside this place, and laughs even more when she realizes that she will be probably the one teaching them shortly. They are good people and hard workers, but they lack experience. She can teach them well, but they will need to work until their backs ache if they want to be even close to the level of any master chef in the City.

But even the chef in that kitchen was unable to bake cookies as good as the ones they were enjoying right now. And their faces, while they were eating in silence, was the best response and seal of approval she could ask from them.

Her feet were hurting more than usual, probably as a result of walking so many times between the freezer, the table, and the delivery carts; but she wanted this order to be perfect in all the details. There was a sense of familiarity embed in the note that the nurse left on her nightstand that grabbed her attention, and the little coupon affixed with a paper clip to the note was enough motivation for her to feel special about this request in particular.

She thought about the little machine for her feet, waiting under her bed, and she laughed thinking how much she hated the noise it produced, but also how much she loved the way she was able to sleep after using it for a few minutes every night.

"If only they had invented one device like that for my tired heart!" – she was remembering the latest event that made her decide to move permanently to the hospital. It was a good scare, and she didn't want to have another one living where she was living before. At least here she would get immediate attention if needed.

And on top of that, being in here she was sure she would be alright and nothing bad will happen to her – hopefully for a very long time - given the amount of love coming her way in the form of little heart-shaped red stickers on the corner of each card delivered to her, recharging her soul and spirit with full bars every time she got a new one placed on the cork squares next to her door.

Three Zero Seven

At first, it was like being inside a small armoire with barely enough space to move. He could feel something pressing his entire body, except for his face. It felt warm and soft, similar to one of those blankets that are specially made for a newborn – those that are always white with blue lines on each side -, but big enough to utterly cover him from head to toes. He wanted to stand up, even that he was still trapped in his dream; he wanted to say something, yet his throat was a piece of badly used sandpaper; he wanted to see around, however, the room was dark and filled with silence. He stayed quiet for a few seconds while his brain was making an effort trying to determine exactly where he was. Just the same as the case with his body, apparently his sanity was still walking between the clouds.

Something he noticed right away was the presence of several bursts of light patterns dancing right in front of him. He was decidedly confused at first and tried to find an explanation to what he was seeing, but his brain was having an incredibly hard time processing the scarce data that it was narrowly collecting. He tried to move his head around and noticed something that he was barely able to identify as a hard pillow was forcing him to stay in the same position. He couldn't hear anything either, and so he decided to stay put a little longer and let his memory attempt to come back on its own.

He wasn't sure how long he stayed immobile and in silence, but it felt like a very long time had passed already when he tried to move again in an attempt to see what was going on around him.

"Phosphenes!" – he thought all of a sudden, remembering the name that was given by the scientists to those patterns of light one sees when we close our eyes. The question now was why was he seeing those patterns if he has been keeping them open all this time? Maybe it was just his mental state trying to make a joke on him. Maybe he was daydreaming or having hallucinations. Or maybe, there was a simpler explanation to this.

Slowly, he opened his eyes.

The room was quiet, organized and clean. Actually, way too clean and tidy as far as he could see. There were just his bed, an empty chair and an open closet by the entrance door. There was no nightstands or lamps, no clothes or bags, and not even a radio or a clock. The walls had no frames, pictures, calendars or anything else. They were entirely nude and pale, without any trace of color all around. He was now able to move his head a little bit to each side and noticed that there was an open window to his left but it was night outside; there was no light coming in, not even from the street lights. The bed was comfortable and he felt no pressure points at all under his body. His hands were extended at his sides, but he was unable to move either of them. His legs felt like they both have been sleeping for a while.

He had a subtle desired to move, yet he abandoned the idea almost immediately. Why the rush to react, if he was feeling restful in that position? There was no more pain, no permanent stress or killer cramps to complain about. And besides, there was nobody else in there to help him out in case of need for a spare hand.

This last thought was weird enough to spare him a moment of clarity in the middle of the ever-increasing confusion he was feeling.

"Where is everybody" – the silence around him was now filled with a strange sense of abandonment. It was not supposed to be like this. It was supposed to be festive. He wasn't expecting any type of music, of course, but it was *at least* expected to be confronted with a lot of conversations from plenty of people, almost at the same time, for sure. Did everybody forget the date? Did she forget about the whole plan after all those nights they talked about, and especially after all of her non-stop complains, suggestions and changes?

"Where is she?" – that sounded like a more important question to ask. She was not in there, standing next to him or sitting on the chair.

"Maybe she's sitting outside, reading one of her books thinking that I am sleeping or still under the

effects of the medication. Or she went for a coffee, perhaps".

He called her name several times but there was no response at all. The room stayed quiet and lifeless.

He closed his eyes for a moment to think about a possible explanation that could bring some light to why there was nobody with him, chatting and asking questions about his state. He forgot for a moment that the colorless walls and the empty closet next to the entrance were something out of the ordinary given the circumstances and that the absence of light from the open window at his left was not a common occurrence. His mind was distracted trying to find out why she was nowhere to be seen. There was always a little handwritten note left on the side table when she needed to attend an errand, telling him at what time she was out, and an approximated time when she would be back. But there was not even a side table this time, much less a note from her.

He felt a little spark of electricity running thru his spine that ended in a clicking sound inside his head. He was so confused by this that it took a very long time for him to notice the sounds of voices now talking next to his bed.

He opened his eyes again and looked around in astonishment.

He was able to identify only a couple of them; the person giving instructions to everybody else, and the one standing by the side table next to his bed, holding a red bag with a white and blue logo on the side. He has seen them before coming to his room to check on the machines connected to his body and to review the results of the paper tape that one of the devices was continuously printing out from a small aperture on the front, filled with curved lines going up and down. Given the jumps and bumps he was feeling on his chest, it was easy to assume that it was tracking the status of his heart, dancing like there was no tomorrow to worry about. The rest of the group was formed by new faces, although they were wearing matching uniforms and were moving like a well-trained team, giving each other enough space to work without interference. And they were acting quite fast moving around the room.

There was a lot of loud and clear noises distinctly perceptible: small motors running coming from the printer, beeping and buzzing from the digital equipment placed next to his bed on a mobile cart, people talking, tools being moved from place to place. Everything happening looked like a very well organized chaos. But he was worried for something else, something that caught his attention for a few seconds when he was still trying to understand what was going on: she was sitting on a chair, outside the room, in silence. He saw her thru the door when one of the team members walked out and another person kept the door open for him. She was sitting with her hands between her legs, fixedly looking at the floor. But she didn't look worried at all. She was in the same position he has seen her taking every time she needed time to process something that was bothering her, especially after a jump. She was immersed in her thoughts, apparently not paying any attention to what was going on around her. Or maybe this was her way to take notice of the mayhem inside the room.

She looked focused, disconnected from reality, embedded in her inner world, far away from this place and this time. But he knew her better. He was sure she was ingesting everything at an accelerated rhythm; she was like that all the time. He was worried only for a bit of a second, and then realize that there was nothing to be concerned about her. If there was something for sure in between all of this, it was that she was keeping her thoughts under control. She was a trained master in the legendary art of *"I can take care of myself"*. He had learned a lot about self-control and governance of the surrounding environment just by listening to her after coming back from one of those now-famous scares, back in their time. She was always giving him very precise instructions to follow and steps to take and was quick to identify errors and correct him if anything was not as she expected it to be. He decided to close his eyes again and to try to do the same, although he was certain he will fail miserably as every other time he tried. But he slowly closed them anyway.

The beeping and buzzing from the machines was the first thing to go silent, and then the whirring from the printer talking to his heart. The clank of the tools changing location was no longer audible either. He was still listening to the voices though, but they were slowly fading away until they became just a whisper, barely perceptible against the sounds that were coming from the side where the window was located. He wasn't paying enough attention to the rest of the room when he was trying to figure out what was going on, but a very specific detail that he noticed before about the windows was that it was closed before, while the team was working around him. How was now possible that he was able to hear all the noises coming from the outside?

He opened his eyes, but by the time he did that the voices were all gone too. A fresh breeze was moving the curtains and the room was empty except for his bed, the chair, and a TV set that he didn't saw before, hanging from the wall above one of those high tables that are used to serve and eat food while staying in bed. The TV was turned off, but this little detail didn't bother him at all. He was trying to see how this could be happening, and the fewer distractions he could have, the better the chances to concentrate on the task at hand he would have.

The silence was a welcome change. He preferred this to the chaos caused by the team and the noises of the machines, although she was again no longer around. Was he going in and out of a hallucination episode? The switch between scenes was too fast to be a dream or even to be the result of the sudden awakening after a dream.

This changing of rooms every time he closed his eyes was without any question intriguing and mysterious, but he was completely and utterly unable to point out a valid and reasonable explanation to what was happening to him. The silence that was surrounding the room now was very helpful with his concentration efforts, but he was not sure how long this "peace" will last.

The only thing that he noticed was that he could blink normally and the scene stayed the same, without change. It was only when he felt the spark of electricity on his neck and stayed with his eyes closed for a long time that he "jumped" between the two cases.

He started to question the status of his mental health almost immediately after recognizing this reality.

III

Something he was certain about was the fact that she was alright. He could tell she was in control every time he saw her sitting outside the room with her hands between her legs. It was him who was trying without success to remain calm. The continuous switch between a silent room and the pandemonium caused by the members of the team was starting to get into his nerves. The sparks on his spine and the clicks on his head were a major contributor to his state of mind too. Why was he seeing two different scenarios? And why was he unable to stay in just one? He would have preferred to stay longer in the quiet room since it gave him a space to think, but every time he was there, he started almost immediately to feel uneasy, just by thinking on her. And he was able to see her only when he was seeing the team working around his bed, in between the chaos, although she looked like untouched by it.

"How can she be so damn calm?" – it was one of the myriads of questions he asked himself about her almost since they meet for the first time. He was not like that at first, but she taught him well. And the reason she gave him was quite exquisite: *"only one of us can run at a time, while the other observes and stays close for control, but watching from outside"*.

He didn't understand that at first when he attested to some of the jumps, but then the force of repetitive experiences made him a subject matter expert pretty soon.

He was opening his eyes again to the silent scene when he noticed a fainted image to his side that was not there before. There was quietude around the room, but somebody was now sitting next to him, embracing his head and holding his hand on his chest, while looking directly to his eyes with an expression of compassionate understanding, as if being well aware of what was happening to him. For a moment, he forgot the continuous jumps and focused his attention on his new companion.

"And there she was, with lyrics running across her arms that he could read every day without fatigue. There she was with her hair on fire and her soul dancing inside his mind. And there he was, amazed and surprised with her beauty – even more than before – her charm and her spirit, trying to keep cool while dying from the burning sensation she always causes inside of him".

He loved that poem, and he remembered it every time he was looking at her from a distance.

Why was he seeing her now? Not that he wanted to complain about it, but it was somehow spooky after not seeing anybody else when the room became silent. There were no machines making noise, or tools being moved around. The team was not on view.

It was just him and her.

The breeze was cold, and the wind kept moving the curtains in a rhythm that was an invitation to meditate. He was feeling better now, and the hand that she had over his chest was helping him with controlling his breathing. There was no confusion running wild on him this time. He didn't want this switch to end and when the spark on his spine was back he stayed with his eyes wide open as much as he could. The effort was bigger than he imagined, but he was able to stay in the same situation, with the same conditions in the room, and with her company by his side. It seemed like he was finally gaining some control over his abnormal situation after all.

He looked at her and noticed a tear running from her left eye down her cheek. This simple fact caught him by surprise because he was unable to remember when was the last time he saw her crying, as she was always as solid as an old walnut tree. He recalls every time they had to go to the hospital for multiple reasons, and how she was always cold and in control, without a trace of sadness on her face even if they were embracing bad and terrible news. He remembers the multitude of times when life threw a brick at them and made both to lose balance. She was the one telling him how to get back on track.

Why was she crying this time *while looking directly at him*? He was almost certain she cried before, but never in front of somebody else. She was extremely reserved in that matter and preferred to go somewhere else before letting anybody see her in that state, including him.

He wanted to ask why was she doing that, but he didn't want her to leave. He was feeling great now that she was sitting next to him, making the situation a little less disturbing.

His hands were still resting on his chest, with her hands placed on top. He wanted to move them to touch her face, to run his fingers thru her hair, to give her a pinch on the cheek or the nose. To let her know how delighted and amazed he was by having her company in that silent room. But her hands were not moving at all, and he stayed in the same position as before. He looked at her and tried to say the same with his eyes, and he failed miserably. She just smiled but didn't show any sign that the message he was trying to relay was received.

She got closer to him and whispered a few words on his ear with a serene voice, barely perceptive but with enough volume and tone to make him tremble to his core.

"I envy you because I know exactly where the fuck you are going..."

IV

One by one, a multitude of memories were coming back thru his mind in a continuous parade of images, sounds, and even aromas. They were in complete disorder at first, and then they started to follow a chronological array inside his head once he started to focus on them, one by one.

He was looking from the distance, her standing next to the mailbox while he was waiting for the kids to board the school bus he was driving at the time. A few months have passed already but he was still unable to bring his sorry soul to introduce himself to her. It was not that he was shy or something like that, but her presence was that of somebody you would not want to mess with. Even that she was shorter than him, he felt small and weak on those short moments when they crossed their paths at the Plaza.

He remembered the fresh bouquet of roses he brought the first time he knocked on her door and the way his car smelled for a couple of days due to the rose that fell under his seat. He didn't bother to remove it for a few days because that smell was a delicate reminder on how their first encounter was.

He saw her getting genuinely mad at him when he hit the neighbor's dog with his car. He didn't understand at first why was she so angry, until he learned that she gave that dog to them several years before the accident, after rescuing him from a killing shelter. It was a little under two years old when she gave it to them, and they kept it for over a decade afterward.

He saw her jumping after a run; the chaos inside her mind and the sense of being lost on her eyes. He was right there to hold her hand and grab her by her waist while walking back home. He placed her quietly on their bed without a word, and without a complain. She was always very specific on her indications to him.

Kids, relatives, school events, parties, vacations, workdays, sickness, Holidays; all of them coming one by one as lose pages from an old scrapbook. He was reading them again, word by word while she was keeping her hand on his chest, moving it in rhythm with his breathing. All those moments in life, running through his mind in a symphony of colors, sounds, laughs, songs, tears, laughs and complains. She always in control of her emotions; he always felt lucky to have her by his side.

He started laughing when he recalls the events that ended with her keeping a Magic eight-ball inside the top drawer of her desk at work. He didn't know that but according to her account of what happened, it was extremely helpful with very important decisions while she was in charge, although he always imagined this was one of the best keeping secrets for her and her co-workers, even to this date. He wonders if the ball is still around.

He saw the kitchen and the envelope that changed their lives forever in just an instant. Although they were prepared, they were never *completely prepared* for it.

He saw the window and the red coffee can on top of the stove, with the brown plastic cap and the old label on the front that you could rip for a discount offer on your next buy. He remembered having a few of those coupons in the drawer next to the fridge, but he couldn't say if he used all of them already by the time they left that home.

He saw her expression when they both read the letter, and the first thing she said to him afterward.

He saw every other jump of hers, the actions that were taken by him and her words after coming back from each one of them. He has lost count some time ago, but there were plenty. And he was always worried. She was strong, but he was apprehensive about how strong in reality she was. She was delicate to his eyes, as a rose in the middle of a field, next to a busy freeway running out of town. She was always the first to say that everything was ok, but sometimes – just occasionally – he was not entirely sure about that.

This last thought caused him to feel really bad when he started to remember the time when her father lost his battle with Life, and how this affected her entire existence. She spent a good deal of time visiting him and staying with him while he was taking his strongest medication, just to be sure he was alright afterward. They made it a tradition for her to bring a book from her collection to read it to him. It was always a different book with every visit and never brought one that formed part of a series. Her explanation was never clear, but he assumed that she didn't want to start something she may or may not be able to finish.

He remembers his first times going to her home, and how he looked at the bookshelf in her living room, full from floor to ceiling with a multitude of books, magazines, and atlas of the world.

He feels terrible when he remembers the empty space on the left side of the third shelf from the bottom, four spaces from the edge, and the sole book sitting on the table next to the reading lamp, clearly marked with a "V" on the spine. It is of the same color and design as the other four that are located right before the void. She was never able to put it back to where it belongs after her dad passed away.

They stayed in silence for a while just looking at each other's eyes. Her hands still on his chest, holding him down.

He feels apprehensive now, and he just wants to touch her hair.

V

The sound of chaos was back. The team was running around again and the printer chatting with his heart was back to life, producing lines with an erratic zigzag pattern on them. She was sitting outside still with her hands between her legs, slowly rocking her body back and forth, apparently trying to focus her mind on something important. He wasn't sure if she was even thinking about him, although he knew that she always had a thought for him, at any time, even if her mind is busy with any other topic on hand.

He could see everybody and everything happening around the room. He could hear every voice and every sound. He could understand what they were saying, but he was not paying any special attention to any of the multiple conversations going on at the same time. He was amazed by the coordination of the people attending the scene, and the myriad of small actions being taken by each member of the team in perfect coordination between each other. They were professionals, there was no doubt about it.

But what were they doing specifically, after all?

He crossed his legs and used his hands to rest his head, having his elbows resting on the inside of his thigs. He felt a pinch on the back of his neck like the ones he felt before, but the scene didn't change this time, even after slowly blinking several times. He continued seeing the dance around the bed while he was absorbed in the movements of everybody. Some team members walked outside and came back with additional devices, and then connected them to the power outlet located under the window sill. They started displaying a similar image like the one being generated by the printer, but now directly on three monitors connected to them. One of the persons that brought the equipment started playing with the multitude of dials and buttons that they had until the images were perfectly clear in every one of them.

"Maybe they ran out of paper, perhaps?" – he thought after noticing that they turned the printer off. A Doctor walked in and reviewed the graphs now being displayed on the screens, compared them to the last piece of paper that was generated by the printer and walked away. He didn't say anything to anybody but nodded affirmative to the person standing next to the window, like giving his approval for the switch.

He felt a cramp in his legs and tried to extend them out. His neck felt rigid because he barely had moved for some time. His hands and feet were feeling cold, and his eyes were trying to close by themselves one more time. But he was immersed in the chaos.

He didn't notice at first and took him some serious time contemplating his surroundings and understanding the space until he realizes that he's sitting on the chair, now located by the open closet. He does not remember how or when he moved from the bed onto this chair, and an uneasy and disturbing feeling invades his mind. He's scared now. Amazingly scared.

Barely moving, he turns around and sees if he can make some sense of the situation. Everybody is busy attending either a machine or a section of the bed; everybody is focused and occupied on something; everybody is working. But nobody is attending to him; nobody has their focus on that chair. It's just him, sitting down now with his legs extended and his arms supporting his weight by the sides. Why is he there? He retracts his legs afraid of causing somebody to trip over with them. He opens his eyes wide and turns his head side to side. His heart rate goes faster with every passing second, and the pumping of his blood resonates on his temples. He has never been so afraid about anything in his whole life.

"What's going on?"- he asks with a very weak voice – *"what am I doing sitting here?"* – but either everybody is too busy to pay any attention to his questions, or they can't hear his voice at all. They are just hurrying whatever they are doing, working close to his bed.

It is at this moment when he suddenly realizes that the whole team is attending to him, who is still laying on the bed, immobile. But he's sitting on the chair, looking at them and listening to their conversations. *"How's that even possible?"* - he asks himself, as he grows increasingly confused and disoriented. He tries again to ask them, but they are not listening to him at all.

He keeps watching as they go thru a multitude of tests, connects more cables to his body and checks every screen while they extract syringes and little bottles with liquids in a myriad of colors from a couple of bags placed on top of the side table, and then inject them into the plastic receptacle at the top of the IV line, covered with a small blue cap. It is indeed fascinating to see them in action, although he's is not sure what's happening to *him* that caused them to come over and do what they are doing now. He was feeling alright before the pain started on his neck. It feels now like that happened a long time ago, but he's almost certain that all probably started just after midnight, and that it has been like this only for a couple of hours, maybe three. He hasn't been paying attention to the pass of time, and the only moment when he was actually with the capacity to *think* anything about all of this was when the room was in complete silence. But there was no clock around to check what time it was.

He's feeling worn out with so many switches between chaos and quietude. He just wants to go back to her. He may be still sitting with him in the other room.

Carefully, listening to how the room goes from a jungle into a desert, he closes his eyes one more time, with his hopes placed on seeing her face at least one more time.

VI

"Your soul has been broken so many times, it's getting harder for you to put it back together after a new scare" –. This was a different way to see it, and according to the letter from one of his oldest friends, it was just a sincere effort to help with getting them out from their latest episode. Although the note was specifically directed to him, he could swear his friend was instead talking about her. But this time, it was he who was making the jumps, although against his will.

He looked at her by turning his head until their eyes were right in front of each other's point of view, remembering every single time they grew closer after a dispute. She was looking back at him in silence, maybe thinking about the same situations, given the smirk she had on her lips. It was always a continuous fight, a walk - not in a straight line from one block to the other but rather in a continuous zigzag - barely touching the edges of the path. He remembers the first time he saw her doing that, and how instead of asking questions or condemning her actions, he simply started walking along while holding her hand, singing a song to try to soothe her soul.

She got up from the bed but kept her hand on his chest for a little while. He was feeling a great comfort with that, and when she tried to move it away he took it with his own and placed it back on the same spot.

She understood and stayed by his side without saying a word, and just smiling at him. It was a little odd for them to stay like that for a moment or two, given that they both were very talkative most of the time. There was never a dull moment when they were together, always with something to talk about. It could be an open discussion related to the latest movie they just saw, or a friendly conversation with no topic in particular while they were enjoying a night out. He was the one hoarding the chat most of the time, but she never complains since she enjoyed listening to him, and especially when he started to narrate one of his adventures from when he was young.

He moved his mouth briefly but the volume of his voice was not enough for her to catch what he was trying to say. She got closer and asked him to repeat what he just said to her. He grabbed a few strands of hair that were hanging by her nose and placed them back behind her ear. Her eyes were wide open while his own eyes were barely perceptible, but he was able to see her perfectly fine. He took a deep breath and repeated what he said before. This time, she understood every single word and pressed her hands even more on his chest.

He was thinking of all the troubles they had, from day one until a few weeks ago. They both had their share of issues that combined caused a bigger one, but they worked their course as a team, as a couple and especially as friends. They never stopped fighting and discussing, but they never forgot to halt everything afterward and share their thoughts on what they did wrong and right. Always a learning experience. They were blessed with a great family, a very loyal group of friends and a multitude of life events worth sharing. Their life book would be a mesmerizing collection of scrap paper, magazine cuts, and handwritten notes all glued together in a rush.

As the graphs on the continuous strip of paper that was coming out of the printer before it got replaced, they had their ups and downs, some closer than others, but every single one of them filled with authentic emotions, incertitude, sureness, and plenty of love.

Everything was clear now: the jumps, the chaos when he was sitting on the chair in one moment and the silence when he was laying on the bed in the next. It was confusing at first, but the time he spent during the moments when the window was open and the breeze was moving the curtains helped him to fully understand what was going on for certain and in particular what was going to happen to him. He was able to see what the team was doing and why she was sitting outside with her hands between her legs. Something very clear to him was the fact that her face might be the last thing he would ever see, now that she was standing next to his bed, and he was feeling again one of those sparks in his spine.

He started to think in retrospective, remembering his doubts when he saw her for the first time, standing next to the mailbox. He was recalling the questions he got from his friends about his plans, the conversation he had with himself almost every night and in particular every time she was walking the forest behind the ranch, after a rainy day in May. There were so many things that could have to happen in a very different way as they did, and some many others that never saw the light of day.

He sees himself at the kitchen table, having a coffee while saying goodbye to the kids. He sees her walking back from the mailbox and sitting next to him without even turning or looking to where he is.

"It was worth it" – he said, letting her hand go, keeping his eyes on hers while closing them slowly, now for the last time.

VII

His hand is no longer strong enough to hold hers. It's not even moving. It's cold and pale like it has been since the early hours when he said goodbye to her. But she keeps holding it while she tells him how much she loves spending the time together. She remembers the time when it took him almost the whole night just to build enough courage to come closer to her and to ask for a dance when they found each other at a party. She remembers that she said no and walked home alone. He came back the next week with flowers in one hand and a basket of dried fruit in the other, knocked on her door and said "Hi" as if nothing happened. She remembers how they spent one of their first dates sitting by her porch eating fruit and talking about why he brought her flowers. She tells him the same story again, on how he convinced her about his good intentions just by walking to her door that day. And how they were inseparable after that.

She's feeling lost and knows very well that later on, the void will try to overrun her brain and will try to convince her one more time that she didn't do enough to help him; that she could have lent him her wings to support his drained spirit and depleted body. And she will pay just enough attention to feel her insides getting colder and empty as she descends into the abyss of her doubts and lack of confidence. She knows very well how hard this time it will be, given that he will no longer be to her side to whisper those words that made her react when she was about to jump, long time ago. This time, new encouraging words will need to come from her inner self.

She stands up and looks at the man that once promised to take care of her forever and thinks how the roles were reversed for the past few months. She is feeling a little better now, thinking that his strange request was fulfilled to the last single detail. Everybody cooperated in good spirit. Everybody forgot the differences between each other and their arguments for a moment. They all wanted to laugh and have some time with the old man again. And oh boy how they did just that.

The team from downstairs came to the room and snapped her out from her moment with him as they knocked at the door. They are very sorry to disturb her, but they need to start their work already. She fully understands, cleans her eyes with the back of her hand and walks in silence; turns back to see her husband while he rests peacefully on his bed with no more machines connected to his beaten body, and without a cup of coffee or a cookie between his hands. His face tells the story of somebody that lived a full life, surrounded by his family even if they were not on the same home at the same time.

"She's been looking for a smile to match her own; she's been searching for a sign that gives her hope. And after all these many years she finally found what she's been looking all around" – the song starts on her head without any effort from her part.

It was playing on the radio the first time they went out as a couple, and become their favorite since then – *"He's been waiting for a song to soothe his soul; he's been hoping for a dance that moves his bones. And after all these many years he finally found what he's been looking all around"*.

He always said that it was the perfect reflection of their symmetrical nature.

She looks at him, blows a kiss, turns around and quietly closes the door behind her.

One

The explanation given to them from the beginning was quite simple, after all, and made total sense to her. Still, she wasn't sure why she felt a great discomfort with the whole idea. Was it envy what she was feeling at that moment? A false sense of failure, perhaps? Whatever that could have been, it was definitely out of place. She forced herself to discard any negativity from her thoughts and instead, continued checking out the special shelf where most of the greeting cards were displayed at the store.

The gift shop was small but well stocked with all the necessities for a last-minute stay. They had a section with lots of snacks and drinks, newspapers, some books and popular magazines. She imagined how many people could look for something to read while waiting for news, just to keep their mind occupied. For her, writing was a preferred method to scape reality: short stories, poems, songs or maybe some loose quotes that could form part of a book later on. She was always carrying a small black composition notebook on her bag, filled with a multitude of parts from her lifeblood.

She found a little "Thank You!" card with the image of a reddish orchid on the front. It looked like it was hand-painted, with touches of a transparent varnish at the tip of each petal. This caused the image to reflect the light from the window in a form that simulated the effect of dew droplets when she moved the card sideways. She liked this little detail a lot, pondering if whoever created that image, added the varnish with that intent, or if this was the result of a very lucky coincidence. She noticed a few traces along the flower's stem that could be the artist's signature and took a picture to look after it later on. The flower was drawn in front of a modernist design composed almost exclusively of black lines crossing in all directions over a white background. It looked like the patterns that are formed on the floor when you take a brush out of a can of paint without scrapping it first on the edge. She let loose a giggle thinking on how that image was a perfect representation of the state of her mind at that moment. Or at any given moment for that matter. Grabbing a matching envelope from a bin next to the shelf, she walked towards the counter where she placed the card not before taking a dark chocolate bar from a box at her left side. Sugar comfitures were one of her oldest and most reliable friends.

"Do you mind if I ask you who you will be giving this card to?" – the question took her by surprise, but the young woman attending the cash register asked very politely and with a sincere smile on her face. She looked like if she were expecting a very specific response to her inquiry.

"...not at all, of course" – she answered after a few seconds of silence from her part. She was still

unrolling from her chaotic state of mind and hasn't spoken to anybody else since she left his room this morning.

"It's for the old woman in the kitchen. She helped me with a special order and just wanted to say thank you for making it possible, given the time…".

"I know her! Well, we all do. She's amazing!" – the girl pressed a couple of buttons on the cash register and the cost of the card was reduced from a little over five dollars to just $2.99. She noticed the question marks on her eyes – *"Employee's discount"* – she said with a smirk. She then opened a drawer and extracted a roll of stickers shaped in the form of little red hearts. She took one of them and motioned it towards the top right corner of the card without applying it. At least not before asking for permission.

"She will like this if that's ok with you" – her eyes were shining under the white light lamp over her head – *"We always do it for cards intended for her, and especially if it is a pretty 'Thank You' card like yours"*.

"Sure. Go ahead" – She was not paying enough attention, focusing more on getting the money from her purse, rather than asking or wondering the reason for the sticker.

"Maybe a tradition, or an internal joke" – was the only explanation that came from her brain but said

nothing aloud. She paid the receipt and walked away after thanking the young girl behind the counter.

She opened the main door to the street and felt the freshly light breeze touching her face. It's been a few hours already since the last time she went out, as she was busy attending to all the visitors they had. The Sun was showing on top of the trees that were lined up on the right side of the parking lot, and the reflection of its light on the clouds was making a fantastic effect with colors and shadows forming a lovely pattern. She was always a fan of this time of the day when the temperature is just right, the wind is gentle and the mayhem of a regular day is yet to be unleashed. The only thing that was missing was a cup of coffee and a piece of Tiramisu cake.

Well, there was more that was missing. But for her surprise – and given the circumstances - she realizes that she was indeed feeling hungry.

That part of the Plaza was always silent in the mornings, even with people running or walking on the track that goes around by the edges almost entirely covered by the shadow of the trees; most of them wearing earplugs and dangerously paying no attention at all to their surroundings. The street vendors were already busy unpacking and preparing themselves for the peak hour at noon while most of their customers were right now still immersed on checking emails, attending meetings and surviving with only coffee or tea.

The Lake at the right side was comparable to a natural sanctuary visited by a very diverse collection of birds all-year-around, and the 25 cents feeders installed by the local zoo all along the small dock was the preferred hot spot for them. Visitors from out of state and locals alike loved to experience taking selfies and videos feeding the animals and the city loved the contributions that were collected from the vending machines every day. The teachers from the Elementary School located a couple of blocks away on the west side have come to form a tradition out of walking their kids to this location every year to learn about eco-systems, fish, plants and everything in between since it was built, a long time ago. They were always trying to make this visit something unforgettable for their students, and with the help of the City employees and a multitude of young volunteers attending from the Local Community College, these visits have been always carried out with safety, loaded with interesting information and filled with lots of games and fun times.

An abundance of benches located at the left side of the lake formed a different type of sanctuary, mostly occupied by middle-aged people reading books, youngsters working on their homework or studying for their tests and retirees enjoying a fresh cup of coffee to go while reading the newspaper. Old school mixed-up with new tech, some would say. There were no feeders installed on this zone, but the birds made their nests on the multitude of great tree branches that hang over the lawn precisely because of the absence of chaos. It was always a pleasure for anybody to sit here, stay for a while and relax in silence, sometimes before going back home after work.

She was still confused about why the girl at the cash register changed the price after asking who the recipient was but pleased with the design of the card. Taking it out from the plastic protective sleeve, she moved it back and forth and watched the effect of the varnish under natural light. It was a piece of art, no doubt about it. She took out her phone and did a quick search on the web for the artist that created it, based on the lines she saw drawn on the flower's stem and found out that she was right on thinking on those traces as a signature. The artist was a young lady from another state and had a page filled with lots of similar pieces of art for sale. She was now thinking of going back later in the afternoon and buy a second card for her. There was an appointment to attend with the Legal department of the hospital anyway, and that gift shop was strategically placed between the front door and the main lobby, just at the right distance from the cafeteria.

The water on the lake was moving with smooth waves as gusts of wind were coming running from under the bridge. Her hair was now a mess, and she started to feel cold despite the sun shining high all across the park. Maybe it was not the weather what was causing her sudden discomfort, but rather the urge to run crawling all along her spine. Her white knuckles, the closed fists and her rattling teeth were a vivid reminder of the fury she felt every time she came back from an episode, feeling like a rag doll tossed away face down in the middle of the road during a storm. There have been no jumps for a very long time, but the desire to look down from the highest point was always an ominous presence on her life. She started reliving the past weeks on her mind, going thru every decision they made and how everybody was planning to handle closure in their own terms. She needed to come to terms with life, and the sooner the better. Especially now that she would not be hearing encouragement cheers from her teammate. Or at least not in an audible form.

Her decision to walk to the park proved its worth against the alternative to just stay and sit down in the little lobby next to the man's bathroom, next to the elevators.

Her brain, heart, and soul all needed a break, and her lungs were happy with the fresh air. She took a pen from her bag and started writing inside the card.

It was hard at first, but then the words and ideas commenced to flow the same as the water in the Lake, forming one wave after the other in slow succession. She was grateful with the way her request was promptly managed and how it was delicately delivered to his room. The rusty old cup was placed front and center and seeing his surprised expression when he saw it was worth the ticket by itself. And the kids truly loved the cookies, probably even more than the rest of their food, given the mess they did on the floor.

She is certain that this was simply one more job for them, but one where anybody could tell they paid enough attention to all the details on every single dish included. No wonder everybody loved that woman so much, as the girl in the gift shop told her.

Finishing with her note inside of the card, she put it again inside its protective plastic cover and inside her handbag, signed and ready to be delivered.

The little red sticker on the corner was, as a matter of fact, a very nice touch.

III

Legal matters were never her strongest asset, but fortunately for both, he was always a planner, thinking in advance whatever was needed for the benefit of both. And they got just barely enough time to discuss, decide and leave his business in order. It's amazing how 25 weeks feel like rush hour at the train station located downtown when you're in a race against time, with no other possible outcome than the one they already expected since the beginning.

She was getting nervous while still sitting down at the desk, signing documents and heavily thinking that her apanthropy was probably going to start knocking at her door at any given moment, but she had learned to control that feeling when they started a family, and now it was just a dim and distant memory on the back of her head. The last papers were reviewed and placed in a folder, and the executive shook her hand while handing her a small portfolio with everything she would need.

Walking down the corridor, she felt a great sense of relief knowing that there were no more details to worry and that his strangest wish was granted. She remembered the moment when he showed her the pamphlet and they both started making jokes about it. But the more she was thinking about it – and especially now that it was in fact becoming a reality – the idea was not that crazy sounding after all. She fought with him at first but came to terms with the concept at the end. And given how pushy he was with it, she had no other choice than accept his terms and plan for it with gratitude.

The music in the elevator reminded her of the first time they went to the movies. The place was almost empty and the popcorn was stale; the seats smelled like urine and the floor was sticky in some areas but slippery in others. They picked the place at random and just walked in without even checking which movie was playing. They choose not to sit down once they saw the conditions of the theatre, and stayed standing up at the back instead. But the smell was stronger than their desire to watch a rerun of an old movie and walked out in laughs.

They were walking around with no particular place to go until they found a taco truck still open in one of the parking lots next to the mall and spent a few hours talking about her jumps, sitting in one of the picnic tables placed in there to eat. The night was genuinely nice, with a full moon and no clouds to cover it. She made a joke about watching out in case he became a werewolf. He knew she was nervous sharing very intimate details of her life with him.

He was deeply intrigued by the reasons behind her jumps but listened to her with an authentic desire to learn. She never felt judged, criticized or looked down by him as she explained how it all started. He was asking a lot of questions, but just so he was clear he was honestly and truly understanding her. At the end of her long explanation, he stood up, grabbed her hands to pull her from the seat and gave her a hug that felt like putting an overcoat on before walking out of the house during a winter storm. They stayed like that for a very long time, with none of them wanting it to end, and felt ephemeral when they finally separated and sat down again, smiling and still holding their hands.

She never said a word about it to anybody. Not friends or family and especially not to him; but this was the exact moment when she stopped feeling hopeless for the very first time in her whole life.

She walked out of the elevator and was about to get thru the main doors when suddenly realize that she was forgetting something really important. She turned around and walked inside the small gift store next to the cafeteria, getting closer to the greeting cards shelf and took one with the red orchid in front of black lines running in all directions over a white background, placing it over the counter together with a matching envelope. The attendant looked perplexed for a few seconds, given that she recognized her when she walked in and asked if the other card got damaged, lost or something else.

"Not at all. I just love the design and wanted one for myself" – she was keeping her eyes directly looking into the counter with her head down, but she lifted it and

asked the young girl about the red heart-shaped sticker she placed on the first card she bought.

"That's our way to tell her that she has us" – the girl noticed her inquiring face – *"She survived two heart attacks almost one after the other a few months ago, and she lives scared of a third one. She moved permanently into the Adult Care section of the hospital but spends her time helping in the kitchen quite often. I think she has worked in some other restaurants downtown, back when she was younger and probably feel like home around cooking and baking. You should come around any Holiday and try one of her cookies. They are amazing. We all love her and want her to stay with us as long as possible. This is how we tell her that"*.

"Little hearts, supporting a bigger one" – she was very pleased with that explanation. There was no employee's discount this time, but she asked for a little sticker and got one for herself.

"Everybody needs a push once in a while" – she thought as she walked out of the store, thinking where she will be placing her card, and directed her steps towards the exit and into the streets.

IV

It was not the same feeling, of course, but that was kind of expected. The kitchen table felt like it was too big for the spacing, although the distance to the walls stayed the same. Maybe it was the location of the chairs or the way the stove was facing the bathroom door. Or maybe, perhaps, it was the sink that looked too big and too tall for the area. She could have found a thousand and one different reasons to explain the void running across the corridors and the emptiness that was undermining her core, forcing her to feel like being out of place after returning home, but then she would be lying to herself. She took way too much time just to insert the key and turn it the first time she arrived from the hospital. She crossed the door's frame and stayed looking around while standing still right in the middle of the living room for what appeared to be an eternity.

It was supposed to be better now, after a few weeks have passed, but the sensation was still the same as it was when she was sitting outside his room, with her hands in between her legs, and listening to all the noise that the team was making while attending the code blue call that night. She wanted to be in control of her emotions but this proved to be harder than she ever expected as she saw them rushing in and out of his room, and especially while seeing him being connected to all those noisy machines with their beeps and buzzing alarms.

The whirring of the printer connected to his heart was deeply getting into her nerves and made her decide to stay outside, instead of sitting down next to him. That decision was something she was unable to forget and probably will be incapable to forgive.

Dropping the bag of groceries on top of the table, she took a knee to the floor to tie up one of her tennis shoelaces that becomes loose while walking outside. Both of her hands touched the floor for a moment and her face was looking down when she had to kneel entirely and sit on her legs under the full weight of her shredded wings. Too many runs had taken their toll on them over time. Pieces of all sizes were hanging from the tips and big holes in between the feathers where the wind has sung its voice with the deepest tone. She was not crying, but her entire body was reacting incontrollable to the anguish and despair that was trying to advance against her will, corroding her inner core with pain and disappointment. It had been a continuous fight lately, and she had endured her battle with great fortitude and resilience. Still, she was in a desperate need to just breathe in peace for a moment or two and to allow her completeness check to finish a full cycle before standing up for one more time. She just needed a break, she told to herself without too much convincing, while filling her lungs and pressing her hands to the floor, pushing her weight up and standing again, grabbing the fridge's door handle for equilibrium.

After a few minutes had passed and her breath was back to normal, she started taking some of the groceries out from the bag to place them inside the pantry. *"Maybe it's time again to pay him a visit"* – she knew it was more of an excuse than a valid reason or need, but the sole idea of talking to him and unpack her entire bag of remorse without complains or resentment was enough of a cause to get her bearings in full march.

It has been a while since the last time she went out. She was extremely aware of that and the episodes were happening more often than desired. She needed to do something to help herself out of that situation. Talking to him was always the antidote she needed to bring her sanity afloat. She didn't want to accept it entirely, but she was finally embracing the fact that he was right with his plan.

The rain was still pouring but it was starting to show signs of fatigue. The first of many school buses were arriving at the stop as she looked thru the kitchen's window to enjoy the same routine she experienced so many times since the first day she moved in when she thought it was a very bad decision for somebody like her to move to a place like this. The kids were not the same, but they were behaving like any others she saw before, jumping out of the bus and running to their homes. Some moms were out on their front yard to greet their children and some stayed inside but looking to them as they got safely at home.

It was a very familiar scene, and she started to revive the countless times she stayed on that same spot, listening to the screams, the running and the warnings asking them to stay out of the street. It was all too familiar. The only thing that was missing was a dog barking while greeting the youngsters, and this little detail was enough for her to stay quiet and tried to listen more carefully but there was none around. This made her feel immensely pissed off, but there was nothing she could do to fix it. At least not for now. Not until she was ready and able to go again to the same shelter as before, she thought with a smirk on her face.

She went upstairs and changed her clothes. It was getting late already and she was still wearing her gym attire when the last school bus had arrived and departed from the stop by the bench next to the mailbox.

V

It was not a bad idea, after all, she had to admit it. The place was beautiful, with lots of trees all around and beds of flowers in between. A small river with pristine waters parted the place in two, but several little bridges allowed visitors to walk across the two sections without trouble. A multitude of birds had made this place their home, and one could spend hours admiring a scurry or two, collecting nuts for winter. The sun was high in the sky and the temperature was perfect for this time of the year. The area where all the new residents were located was one of the most frequently used, for obvious reasons. Here, yellow roses were predominant on the sides of the trails, although there were also carnation, peony, sweet Williams, heliotrope, lilies, and tulips. The grass was of a tone of green that looked like it was painted, perfectly manicured and running up and down across several small hills.

Rare enough for a piece of advertising, the pamphlet he showed her when they were talking about the preparations was indeed a perfect representation of the actual place. The pictures did make justice to the beauty of the area.

She sat down on a bench that faced the South and lifted her head to feel the sun kissing her cheeks. The breeze was fresh enough to secure a hoodie or a light sweater, but not that cold to make one feel uncomfortable while visiting the place. It seems like whoever came up with the idea spent a good deal of time just looking for the perfect spot to start the project. It was not that far away from the City, but far enough to secure a placid experience without the typical noise of the suburbs. The road from the highway exit to the main entrance was well kept and the trip from her home to here was a smooth ride for the entire trip.

He was just a couple of steps away, still small in comparison with the others, but the regular afternoon rain that was common in the area would be a great help in securing his grow. It was weird the first time she did it, but after a couple of visits, it has become natural to speak directly to him as if he was sitting next to her on the bench. Therapeutic in a sense, the way she was surrounded by nature made it way more comfortable and uplifting than the traditional exhibition, very common since the good old days.

"You want to be…what? – she asked in surprise when he was talking about the place while unfolding the pamphlet on the kitchen table, using the salt and pepper shakers as supports to stop it from rolling back.

"Not 'to be', but rather 'to become', if that makes more sense" – he was having a blast containing his laugh while he was feeling amused by seeing the bafflement and confusion reflected on her eyes – *"just*

think about it. A park that is indeed full of trees instead of cold Lapides"

"Life instead of voids and illusion. Green rather than gray. You will love to come and chat, and tell me about your runs, or the lack of thereof"

And he was right. His last mischief, growing right in front of her. Still small and a little weak, but beautiful and full of promises as he always was to her eyes. She looked around seeing the others that surrounded the area and smiled thinking how he will become an identical one in the not so distant future.

She spent a good deal of time just sitting in there, letting her spirit be lifted by the weather, the fresh air and the smell of roses, but she was getting hungry and had to go back home. She took a bag she had next to her and extracted a small cigar box from it. Carefully, like trying not to cause any permanent damage, she opened it and extracted an engraved aluminum plate, painted in black with yellow letters; a small red heart was on the top right corner inside the frame.

One of the most difficult decisions she made when the arrangement took place was to add all of his notes, cards, and letters he gave to her thru the years to the cardboard box where he was placed for processing. She thought that they belonged to him anyway as they were pieces of his heart and soul, and now they were part of the tree too. But she kept one for herself and made it into that plate to place it next to him as a special marker, once he was bigger and stronger. She liked the idea of reading it every time she will come to see him again.

It was just a little handwritten note in a yellow index card that he even didn't write for her, but rather to a friend, a very long time ago. He was answering to his doubts about why he was planning to ask her in marriage.

"I don't love her because she's pretty or because she treats me right, although there is plenty of both. I love her because of the way my demons dance every time she smiles at me from afar".

As he always said about their favorite song after hearing it for the first time, this card was also a perfect reflection of their symmetrical nature. It was only proper to have it installed next to him and to share it with other visitors as a marker of what their lives had become. She had carried the card on her purse for a very long time, and now he will be carrying it too for all the years to come.

She placed the plaque back on the cigar box and then on the bag and stood up in silence, walking towards him. Looking to each of the branches already expanding in all directions she extended her hand and ran her fingers on some of the leaves, remembering several times when he ran his fingers across her hair.

VI

The place was packed, as it normally was on a Friday night. She was hesitant to come at first, but the desire to be in a well-known territory was bigger than her uncertainty about going out by herself. The food here was fantastic, and there were always local bands playing on the covered patio area located at the back. They always preferred a spot inside just to be able to chat without raising their voices more than necessary but still being able to listen to the music if they wanted to enjoy it. Most of the tables had four chairs with them, but there were also several small accommodations by the windows for two or even one single guest, which were normally not used as often as the others.

Staring for a very long time to the people already inside, she recognized some of them just by their looks, although without knowing their names. He was always pointing out very small details about the people around, and she was always smiling while thinking how much attention he was paying to their surroundings all the time. But still, he was a very good listener even if she has nothing to say at the moment.

For him – on his own words as he was describing her during one of their first dates – she was a mystery: *"like an unknown path on the trail that you see every time you go for a hike; and then one day you made up your mind and go left instead of right, walk for hours under the shadows of the trees and start hearing the song of a river. And as you emerge from the forest that was covering your view for most of the trip, you finally have a sighting of what is coming ahead of you".*

She started to feel confused, disoriented, lost, out of senses; doubtful. So many ways to describe it. Not because she didn't know what she was supposed to do, but because she wasn't sure if her heart was in the right place. *"Deja vu"* – she thought as she felt the weight of her wings pressing hard over her shoulders. They were supposed to carry her, and not the other way around.

The hostess was checking the map of the floor as she was picking menus from the basket to her side, and a few seconds later – after greeting her with a smile – asked how many there were on her party.

So many jumps, so many runs. Hesitation at first, faithfulness at the end; solitude and then commitment; silence and quorum. She was a recluse for most of her ambivalence towards life; he was there when she discovered her unwavering resolve.

Her brain was now flooding with memories about the smell at the movie theater, the dog barking to the kids after school, the envelope with her acceptance letter from College and her hesitation to open it, the chocolate chip cookies shared with the whole family, the books on her shelves and the one placed on top of the side table under the reading lamp, the magic eight ball that helped finalize several work projects when needed, the brown cap on the red coffee can – without the discount coupon on the front, of course –, the bench in front of him, and so many more. It was like pouring rain after a very hot day in July. It could have been so different from what it was, in so many ways. But it was worth it. Every single day.

"Yes. Please…" – she started saying as she was still rolling the movie inside her brain while trying to recover from the trip thru memory lane. But she was good; smiling a bit and in control as many times before.

"…yes…" – it was harder than expected, after all. She would need to quickly adjust and at least strive for verisimilitude.

"…table for one".

49at67.com